CW00959057

A Musical

Book by
Michael Bennett

Music by
Cy Coleman

Lyrics by
Dorothy Fields

Based on the play *Two for the Seesaw* by
William Gibson

Written, directed, and choreographed by
Michael Bennett

A SAMUEL FRENCH ACTING EDITION

SAMUEL FRENCH

FOUNDED 1830

New York Hollywood London Toronto

SAMUELFRENCH.COM

Book Copyright © 1975 by Michael Bennett
Lyrics Copyright © 1973 Dorothy Fields

ALL RIGHTS RESERVED

CAUTION: Professionals and amateurs are hereby warned that *SEESAW* is subject to a Licensing Fee. It is fully protected under the copyright laws of the United States of America, the British Commonwealth, including Canada, and all other countries of the Copyright Union. All rights, including professional, amateur, motion picture, recitation, lecturing, public reading, radio broadcasting, television and the rights of translation into foreign languages are strictly reserved. In its present form the play is dedicated to the reading public only.

The amateur live stage performance rights to *SEESAW* are controlled exclusively by Samuel French, Inc., and licensing arrangements and performance licenses must be secured well in advance of presentation. PLEASE NOTE that amateur Licensing Fees are set upon application in accordance with your producing circumstances. When applying for a licensing quotation and a performance license please give us the number of performances intended, dates of production, your seating capacity and admission fee. Licensing Fees are payable one week before the opening performance of the play to Samuel French, Inc., at 45 W. 25th Street, New York, NY 10010.

Licensing Fee of the required amount must be paid whether the play is presented for charity or gain and whether or not admission is charged.

Stock licensing fees quoted upon application to Samuel French, Inc.

For all other rights than those stipulated above, apply to: Samuel French, Inc.

Particular emphasis is laid on the question of amateur or professional readings, permission and terms for which must be secured in writing from Samuel French, Inc.

Copying from this book in whole or in part is strictly forbidden by law, and the right of performance is not transferable.

Whenever the play is produced the following notice must appear on all programs, printing and advertising for the play: "Produced by special arrangement with Samuel French, Inc."

Due authorship credit must be given on all programs, printing and advertising for the play.

RENTAL MATERIALS

An orchestration consisting of **Piano/Conductor Score, Orchestra Parts, and Chorus Parts** will be loaned two months prior to the production ONLY on the receipt of the Licensing Fee quoted for all performances, the rental fee and a refundable deposit.

Please contact Samuel French for perusal of the music materials as well as a performance license application.

No one shall commit or authorize any act or omission by which the copyright of, or the right to copyright, this play may be impaired.

No one shall make any changes in this play for the purpose of production.

Publication of this play does not imply availability for performance. Both amateurs and professionals considering a production are strongly advised in their own interests to apply to Samuel French, Inc., for written permission before starting rehearsals, advertising, or booking a theatre.

No part of this book may be reproduced, stored in a retrieval system, or transmitted in any form, by any means, now known or yet to be invented, including mechanical, electronic, photocopying, recording, videotaping, or otherwise, without the prior written permission of the publisher.

ISBN   978-0-573-68069-4   Printed   in   U.S.A.   #968

SEESAW, a musical. Music by Cy Coleman; lyrics by Dorothy Fields; based on the play "Two For The Seesaw" by William Gibson; setting by Robin Wagner; costumes by Ann Roth; lighting by Jules Fisher; musical director and vocal arrangements by Don Pippin; orchestrations by Larry Fallon; dance arrangements supervised by Cy Coleman; media art and photography by Sheppard Kerman; sound by Dick Maitland, Bob Ring and Lou Gonzales; production associate, Charlotte Dicker; associate choreographers, Bob Avian and Tommy Tune; co-choreographer, Grover Dale; written, directed and choreographed by Michael Bennett; production stage manager, Robert Borod. Presented by Joseph Kipness and Lawrence Kasha, James Nederlander, George M. Steinbrenner, 3rd and Lorin E. Price. At the Uris Theater, New York City March 18th, 1973.

CAST
(*In Order of Appearance*)

JERRY RYAN	*Ken Howard*
GITTEL MOSCA	*Michele Lee*
DAVID	*Tommy Tune*
SOPHIE	*Cecelia Norfleet*
JULIO GONZALES	*Giancarlo Esposito*
SPARKLE	*LaMonté Peterson*
NURSE	*Judy McCauley*
ETHEL	*Cathy Brewer-Moore*
CITIZENS OF NEW YORK	

CAST OF CHARACTERS
(*In Order of Appearance*)

JERRY RYAN
GITTEL MOSCA
DAVID
SOPHIE
JULIO GONZALES
SPARKLE
NURSE
ETHEL
CITIZENS OF NEW YORK

3

SYNOPSIS OF SCENES

The action of the Play takes place in New York City.

ACT ONE

Prologue
 "SEESAW" .... *Full Company*

Times Square Area
 "MY CITY" .... *Jerry Ryan and*
 The Neighborhood Girls

Dance Studio on West 54th Street
 "NOBODY DOES IT LIKE ME" .... *Gittel*

Japanese Restaurant on 46th Street and Lincoln Center
 "IN TUNE" .... *Gittel and Jerry*

East 116th Street
 "SPANGLISH" .... *Julio Gonzales, Gittel, Jerry,*
 Sophie and Full Company

Gittel's Apartment in the East Village
 "WELCOME TO HOLIDAY INN!" .... *Gittel*

Jerry's Apartment
 "YOU'RE A LOVABLE LUNATIC" .... *Jerry*

Gittel's Apartment, then the Street
 "HE'S GOOD FOR ME" .... *Gittel*

The Banana Club
 "RIDE OUT THE STORM" ...... *Sparkle, Sophie and*
 Full Company

Gittel's Apartment

ACT TWO

St. Vincent's Hospital
"WE'VE GOT IT" .... *Jerry*
"POOR EVERYBODY ELSE" .... *Gittel*

Dance Studio
"CHAPTER 54, NUMBER 1909" .. *David, Jerry, Gittel and Dance Company*

Jerry's Apartment

Backstage at the Theatre
"THE CONCERT" .... *Gittel and Dance Company*
"IT'S NOT WHERE YOU START" .... *David and Full Company*

Central Park, later that night

Gittel's Apartment, Phone Booth at Kennedy Airport

Gittel's Apartment, 2:00 AM

Gittel's Apartment, Jerry's Apartment, a few days later
"I'M WAY AHEAD"
"SEESAW" (Reprise) .... *Gittel*

5

Seesaw

ACT ONE

*The CURTAIN rises near the end of the Overture, revealing
a blue-lit Stage. Projections of New York City in black-
and-white Codalith fill the cyclorama.*

*The Cast, all in white costumes, are frozen in the process of
bustling through the city. The CHORUS begins singing.*

CHORUS.
SEESAW
SEESAW
EV'RYBODY'S TRAVELIN' ON A CRAZY
SEESAW
GOING UP . . . DOWN
UP . . . DOWN
SO YOUR LIFE GOES BY
YOU'RE EITHER LOW OR HIGH
ON THE SEESAW
SEESAW
YOU CAN DREAM YOU'LL GO ANYWHERE
YOU WANT TO GO
BUT THAT'S NOT SO
SOMEHOW YOU KNOW
THE TRUTH IS:
NOBODY IS GOIN' ANYWHERE
NOBODY IS GETTIN' ANYWHERE
SO WHAT IF YOU NEVER GET ANYWHERE
IT'S STILL BEEN A HELL OF A RIDE
ONE HELL OF A RIDE!
 (*The SINGERS and DANCERS exit Left and Right.*)
EVERYBODY'S TRAVELIN' ON A CRAZY SEESAW
 SEESAW
EVERYBODY'S TRAVELIN' ON A CRAZY SEESAW
 SEESAW
EVERYBODY'S TRAVELIN' ON A CRAZY SEESAW
EVERYBODY'S TRAVELIN' ON A CRAZY SEESAW
SEESAW SEESAW

(JERRY *enters to PHONE BOOTH Stage Right. He dials.*)

JERRY. Hello, Miss Mosco? Oh . . . well, when is she due back? I see. This is Jerry Ryan. She wouldn't remember. I just got in from Nebraska. Nebraska. I just wanted to say hello. Is there a business number? Could you say it again, I don't have a pencil. 421-7315. Thank you. (*Repeats to himself.*) 421-7315 . . . 421-7315 . . . (*He feels his pockets.*) Now I don't have a dime . . . 421-7315 . . . (*A* MAN *passes.*) Got to get change . . . Excuse me, do you have . . .

MAN. (*Angrily.*) No!

JERRY. Thank you . . . It's nice to be back in New York . . . 421-7315 . . . I'll use a quarter.

(JERRY *goes to PHONE BOOTH, but someone else gets there first. As MUSIC for "MY CITY" starts,* THE NEIGHBOR- HOOD GIRLS *enter from Stage Right and Left, surround* JERRY *and proposition him as he waits for the phone.*)

THE NEIGHBORHOOD GIRLS.
COME ON FELLA, SIT BACK, RELAX, ENJOY
    THE RIDE!
COME ON FELLA, SIT BACK, RELAX, ENJOY
    THE RIDE!
SIT BACK, RELAX, ENJOY THE RIDE!

CHORUS. (*Offstage.*)
THE CITY . . . MY CITY . . .
IS LIKE A BEAUTIFUL WOMAN
BEAUTIFUL . . . THAT'S GOOD
MOST TIMES IMPOSSIBLE . . . THAT'S BAD
SHE TIES ME UP
SHE WON'T LET ME GO EAST
SHE WON'T LET ME GO WEST
I DON'T DARE TO CROSS HER
SOME TIMES I'D LIKE TO TOSS HER
INTO THE RIVER
BUT IF YOU LOVE HER . . . YOU LOVE HER
AND I LOVE MY CITY . . .
I LOVE NEW YORK!

MMMM, MM-MM-MM-MM
MM-MMM-MM!
JUST YOU NAME IT!
WE'LL DIG IT UP FOR YOU!

HOOKERS! HUSTLERS! FRESH FROM EIGHTH
  AVENUE . . .
THE BOOK STORES LOADED DOWN WITH SEX!
MASSAGE PARLORS!
MOVIES RATED TRIPLE X!

AH . . .
JOE'S PIER FIFTY-TWO
THE METROPOLE! HOW WOULD SARDI'S DO?
LIVE MODELS KNOCK YOU FOR LOOP!
A TOPLESS WAITRESS SERVES YOUR ONION
  SOUP!
ALL YOU BOYS WHO COME FROM EV'RYWHERE!
TIMES SQUARE IS LATELY VERY FAR FROM
  SQUARE . . .

The Neighborhood Girls.
COME ON FELLA, SIT BACK, RELAX, ENJOY
  THE RIDE
COME ON FELLA, SIT BACK, RELAX, ENJOY
  THE RIDE
COME ON FELLA, SIT BACK, RELAX, ENJOY
  THE RIDE
COME ON FELLA, SIT BACK, RELAX, ENJOY
  THE RIDE
COME ON FELLA, SIT BACK, RELAX, ENJOY
  THE RIDE.

Women. (Offstage.)
THE CITY . . . MY
  CITY
IS LIKE A BEAUTIFUL
  WOMAN
BEAUTIFUL . . . THAT'S
  GOOD
MOST TIMES
  IMPOSSIBLE . . .
  THAT'S BAD
SHE TIES ME UP
SHE WON'T LET ME
  GO EAST
SHE WON'T LET ME
  GO WEST
I DON'T DARE TO
  CROSS HER
SOME TIMES I'D LIKE

Men. (Offstage.)
JUST YOU NAME IT!
WE'LL DIG IT UP FOR
  YOU!
HOOKERS! HUSTLERS!
  FRESH FROM
  EIGHTH AVENUE.
THE BOOK STORES
  LOADED DOWN WITH
  SEX
MASSAGE PARLORS!
MOVIES RATED
  TRIPLE X!
AH . . .
JOE'S PIER FIFTY-TWO
THE METROPOLE!
  HOW WOULD SARDI'S
  DO?

WOMEN. (*Offstage.*)
TO TOSS HER
INTO THE RIVER
BUT IF YOU LOVE HER
. . . YOU LOVE HER
AND I LOVE MY
  CITY . . .

MEN. (*Offstage.*)
LIVE MODELS KNOCK
  YOU FOR A LOOP!
A TOPLESS WAITRESS
  SERVES YOUR ONION
  SOUP!
ALL YOU BOYS WHO
  COME FROM
  EV'RYWHERE
TIMES SQUARE IS
  LATELY VERY FAR
  FROM SQUARE . . .

CHORUS. (*Offstage.*)
THE CITY . . . MY CITY . . .
IS LIKE A BEAUTIFUL WOMAN
BEAUTIFUL . . . THAT'S GOOD
MOST TIMES IMPOSSIBLE . . . THAT'S BAD
MY CITY . . . MY CITY . . .
AND I LOVE MY CITY . . .
I LOVE NEW YORK . . .
I LOVE MY CITY . . .
NEW YORK!

(*A* COP *enters Stage Left.*)

COP. All right . . . let's move along . . . move along . . .
(COP *crosses to* JERRY *at PHONE BOOTH.*) Didn't you hear
me, fella? Move it! Move it!

JERRY. Officer, I was just waiting to use the phone. (JERRY
ducks into the phone booth and begins dialing, as THE NEIGH-
BORHOOD GIRLS *exit Stage Right.*)

(GITTEL, DAVID *and* DANCE COMPANY *enter Left doing a dance
  combination. Two translucent rehearsal mirrors fly in,
  framing the STUDIO. The desk glides in to Left of
  Center. And the Telephone rings in the STUDIO as*
  JERRY *finishes dialing at the PHONE BOOTH Stage
  Right.*)

GITTEL. (*Making her way through the* DANCE COMPANY *in
the class behind the mirror to the desk, she picks up the
phone.*) Yeah, hello?

JERRY. Hello? Git-tel?

GITTEL. Who?

JERRY. (*Looking at paper.*) Is this Git-tel Mosco?

GITTEL. No, it's Gittel Mosca! . . . Who is this?

JERRY. Jerry Ryan. I'm an old friend of Oscar's. We met a few weeks ago at Oscar's party. Remember? I couldn't hear your name over all that music, so you wrote it down for me, along with your phone number.

GITTEL. Which one?

JERRY. Which number?

GITTEL. No, which one were you? I gave my number out a lot that night . . .

JERRY. Why?

GITTEL. I play the odds. Not everybody calls.

JERRY. *I* called.

GITTEL. You're the only one. See what I mean? . . . Were you the one with the beard or the one with the limp?

JERRY. Both.

GITTEL. Oh, the one with the sense of humor. The Wasp! With the white shirt and the narrow tie.

JERRY. It was my first New York party. I didn't know how to dress.

GITTEL. It was different. You were clean . . . Sure, now I remember. You have that funny way of talking.

JERRY. What funny way?

GITTEL. Nice diction . . . So what's new?

JERRY. Nothing much . . . I just thought I'd call and say hello . . .

GITTEL. Oh . . . Hello . . .

JERRY. . . . Hello . . .

GITTEL. . . . Hello . . . I don't think this conversation has a great future . . .

JERRY. . . . I'm sorry . . . I'm usually not this tongue-tied . . . I just remembered I said I'd call you . . . and I sort of felt obligated to call.

GITTEL. Really? . . . Well, I'm touched more than you'll ever know.

JERRY. . . . That didn't come out the way I intended.

GITTEL. I don't think I want to hear the way you intended.

JERRY. I er . . . I er . . .

GITTEL. . . . Take your time. Work it out.

JERRY. I er . . . just wanted to call and say hello . . . And er . . . I thought you were highly attractive . . .

GITTEL. How high?

JERRY. Very high . . . Oh, hell, I don't know why I called . . . It was nice speaking to you, Git-tel.

GITTEL. Gittel.

JERRY. Gittel.

GITTEL. It was nice speaking to you, Gary.

JERRY. Jerry.

GITTEL. Jerry . . . (*Silence.*) Well, goodbye.

JERRY. Goodbye.

GITTEL. (*A moment.*) Did you hang?

JERRY. I hung. (*He hangs up the phone and exits.*)

GITTEL. Hey, wait a minute! . . . (*She speaks with MUSIC.*)

IDIOT.

IF YOU GAVE THE MAN YOUR NUMBER
AND THE MAN CALLS
AND HE SEEMS A LITTLE NERVOUS AND SHY
YOU DON'T MAKE HIM SHYER OR NERVOUSER
YOU HELP HIM OUT
AT LEAST YOU TRY
OR HE'S JUST GONNA SAY "GOODBYE"
WHICH IS EXACTLY WHAT HE SAID: "GOODBYE"
    (*And she sings.*)

WHEN IT COMES TO MEN
DO I EVER DO WHAT'S RIGHT
ANY YEAR, ANY MONTH
ANY MORNING, AFTERNOON OR NIGHT?

IF THERE'S A WRONG WAY TO SAY IT
A WRONG WAY TO PLAY IT
NOBODY DOES IT LIKE ME
IF THERE'S A WRONG WAY TO DO IT
A RIGHT WAY TO SCREW IT UP
NOBODY DOES IT LIKE ME
I'VE GOT A BIG LOUD MOUTH
I'M ALWAYS TALKING MUCH TOO FREE
IF YOU GO FOR TACT AND MANNERS
BETTER STAY AWAY FROM ME.
IF THERE'S A WRONG WAY TO KEEP IT COOL
A RIGHT WAY TO BE A FOOL
NOBODY DOES IT LIKE ME.

IF THERE'S A WRONG BELL I RING IT
A WRONG NOTE I SING IT
NOBODY DOES IT LIKE ME
IF THERE'S A PROBLEM I DUCK IT
I DON'T SOLVE IT . . . I JUST MUCK IT UP
NOBODY DOES IT LIKE ME
AND SO I TRY TO BE A LADY
I'M NO LADY, I'M A FRAUD
WHEN I TALK LIKE I'M A LADY
WHAT I SOUND LIKE IS A BROAD.

IF THERE'S A WRONG WAY TO GET A GUY
THE RIGHT WAY TO LOSE A GUY
NOBODY DOES IT LIKE ME
NOBODY DOES IT, NO
NOBODY DOES IT . . .
NOBODY DOES IT LIKE ME!

(GITTEL *crosses back to the dance class.*)

DAVID. Okay, okay, learn this. One Two Three Four . . .
(DAVID *does a dance combination.*)
GITTEL. You know what I just lost? A date. With a Wasp.
A half inch taller than you. (JERRY *enters Right to PHONE
BOOTH, dials, and Telephone rings in the STUDIO.* GITTEL
crosses to desk and picks up the phone.) Hello!
JERRY. Gittel!
GITTEL. Yeah!
JERRY. Hello . . . it's Jerry again.
GITTEL. I know. I recognized the hello.
JERRY. S.O.S., Miss Mosca. That means help.
GITTEL. What help? What are you talking about?
JERRY. Very desperate situation, stranger in town sees pretty
girl at party, wants to ask her out to dinner but Miss Mosca
he's afraid of rejections . . .
GITTEL. To dinner? Who says no to dinner? I mean even a
creep you can shake right after the fortune cookies.
JERRY. Then the answer is yes?
GITTEL. The answer is it depends because I gotta know if it's
dinner or *dinner.*
JERRY. What's the difference?
GITTEL. *Dinner* is *dinner,* you know, an hour to fix my hair
and put on a dress, or else it's dinner, I wash my hands and we
eat.
JERRY. I'm afraid it's just dinner tonight.
GITTEL. Oh, fine with me, I hate *dinner,* too many problems
like should I eat the cold soup with a spoon or drink it and
either way I'm wrong because it turns out to be a fingerbowl.
Look, meet me at 46th and Broadway, at eight. Huh?
DAVID. (*From STUDIO.*) . . . Miss Mosca, class!
GITTEL. Look I gotta go, see you later, and don't worry about
your ears I'm not slamming just replacing in haste. Listen.

(*At the STUDIO, PHONE BOOTH,* DAVID, GITTEL *and the*
DANCE COMPANY *clear the stage, we are on 46th and
Broadway. Three rough-looking* MUGGERS *enter Stage*

Right. Two of the MUGGERS *grab* JERRY, *and the* FIRST
MUGGER *holds a gun and reaches for* JERRY'S *wallet.)*

FIRST MUGGER. (*As they quickly exit Stage Left.*) Thanks!
JERRY. (*He looks around, but no one is in sight. Meekly.*)
Officer?
GITTEL. (*Entering from Stage Left, third portal.*) Ahh!
Hiya, Jerry.
JERRY. Hello.
GITTEL. I, ah, hope you haven't been waiting around too
long.
JERRY. Oh no, that's all right. I met some interesting people.
GITTEL. Now . . . what are you in the mood for, Mexican,
Jewish, Japanese, only before you decide, I gotta tell you
Mexican I can't eat, and Jewish is okay but the waiters holler
at you if you leave anything on the plate so that leaves
Japanese, at least it's romantic, you know, empty.

(*During the speech, Screens fly in with projections of a beautiful Japanese restaurant, and a unit glides in with a very
low table and two pillows under it.*)

JERRY. I thought ulcers were a man's disease.
GITTEL. Who do you think I got it from? Hope you don't
mind sitting on the floor. (*They sit,* JERRY *with some difficulty.*)
JERRY. No, no, what do I do with my legs?
GITTEL. Fold em up. You know, like a flamingo.
JERRY. (*Managing to do it.*) All right, Miss Mosca, for you
I'll be a flamingo.
GITTEL. Comfortable?
JERRY. Yes, now you were telling me about your ulcer.
GITTEL. Yeah, we've been going steady for four years. Some
people gotta jump off a roof to kill themselves, all I gotta do
is eat one French fry potato . . . Not that I mind dying, I
mean it's one way to break your lease. (JAPANESE GIRL *has
come up through this.*)
JERRY. . . . Okay, you're the expert, what do we order?
GITTEL. (*Reading from menu on table and playing with
chopsticks.*) I think the bean curd soup for you to begin with,
then sushimi shrimp tempura, and the teriyaki. I'll have a
tuna on rye and a glass of milk . . . (JAPANESE GIRL *starts
to exit.* GITTEL *yells after her.*) . . . and a little rice! (*To*
JERRY.) I love Japanese restaurants, but I hate the food. So
go on, tell me already, where are you from original?
JERRY. Nebraska.

GITTEL. Nebraska? That's somewhere out in California, isn't it?

JERRY. No, I think it's Nevada that's in California.

GITTEL. Nevada, Nebraska. For me the other side of Eighth Avenue is the wild, wild west. I have absolutely no desire whatsoever to travel . . . I don't like planes, trains or boats. If Nebraska wants to come *here*, I'll be glad to say hello.

JERRY. No interest in broadening your horizons?

GITTEL. Now don't give me that. Traveling does *not* make a person smarter . . . if New York doesn't have it, I don't want to see it.

JERRY. That's a very provincial attitude.

GITTEL. I might as well level with you. I'm not smart. My I.Q. is somewhere very close to my temperature . . . without fever. It doesn't embarrass me to tell you because the longer we keep talking, the sooner you'll find out. What's provincial?

JERRY. I'm beginning to think *me* . . .

GITTEL. So how come Nebraska came to New York?

JERRY. Ah, I don't know . . . I guess I just wanted to take a bite out of the Big Apple.

GITTEL. . . . You came here to eat fruit?

JERRY. (*Laughs.*) The Big Apple. New York. It's a local colloquialism.

GITTEL. (*Awed, her mouth drops open.*) Say that again.

JERRY. Local colloquialism.

GITTEL. (*Big smile.*) Jerry, you have earned my respect for life.

JERRY. Would you like me to teach you how to say it?

GITTEL. Forget it. Julie Andrews you can turn into "My Fair Lady" . . . when you're born on Southern Boulevard in the Bronx, that's it for life. I notice you keep looking at the prices . . . Is money a problem?

JERRY. It wasn't until five minutes ago.

GITTEL. Does it help if we go Dutch?

JERRY. It helps you . . . *I'm* still in trouble.

GITTEL. My check, right? Well, it's worth it. Say it again.

JERRY. Local colloquialism.

GITTEL. . . . I could listen to it all night. Does it hurt your tongue?

JERRY. (*Laughs.*) It needs the exercise . . . I've been alone a lot . . . What are you anyway, Italian?

GITTEL. Me? You crazy?

JERRY. Mosca?

GITTEL. Jewish. It used to be Moscowitz.

JERRY. Why'd you change it?

GITTEL. 1 wanted to sound Italian . . . Listen, don't worry about the money. If you're broke, I can lend you . . . I got a milk bottle full of pennies . . . thirty-eight bucks . . . you're the only one I know big enough to lift it.

JERRY. Listen, I think you're getting the wrong idea about me. I'm not a prospect for welfare. I made twenty-eight thousand dollars last year.

GITTEL. You're kidding? . . . My *neighborhood* didn't make twenty-eight thousand last year . . . What do you do?

JERRY. I'm an attorney.

GITTEL. You mean like a lawyer?

JERRY. No, like an attorney. Now don't change the subject, you were telling me how the little Mosca lost its Witz.

GITTEL. (*Not yet knowing how to take him.*) I chopped it off. It was too long for up on the marquee.

JERRY. So you're an actress!

GITTEL. (*Shaking her head.*) Dancer. Jazz! You know . . . (*A couple of finger snaps, head roll, shoulder bump.*) . . . It's better with bongos. (JERRY *laughs.*) What's a matter, I say something funny?

JERRY. No, I just like being with you. You make me laugh.

GITTEL. Laugh how? Ha ha I'm feeling good, or ha ha boy she's a nut I better get the hell outta here . . .

JERRY. Definitely the former. At this moment, Miss Mosca, I am a very happy flamingo . . . (JAPANESE GIRL *has brought steaming bowl of soup, glass of milk and tuna sandwich.*) . . . Aah, that looks good! The bean curd?

GITTEL. Uh-huh. And those little things that look like octopus . . .

JERRY. Yeah.

GITTEL. Are. (*A moment.*) . . . Now let's take our time eating. It took a long time to prepare.

JERRY. (*After a pause.*) How do you know it took a long while to prepare?

GITTEL. I don't. My mother used to say that. It's one of those mother things. I used to save them . . . (*A mother's voice.*) My only wish is when you grow up you'll have a daughter just like you, then you'll know what I go through.

JERRY. That's amazing! My mother said something like that too. Well . . . don't look surprised, we have mothers in Omaha.

GITTEL. Yeah but not like on the Grand Concourse! (*Another one.*) . . . Don't forget to put on clean underwear in case you're hit by a taxi and taken to the hospital I ·don't want to be ashamed . . . (*Short pause.*) How about food? Eat your carrots, they're good for you!

JERRY. Eat your squash, it's good for you!

GITTEL. Eat your octopus, it's good for you!

JERRY. Was there anything that wasn't good for you?

GITTEL. Yeah, hot dogs, Italian ices, anything you liked . . . Geeze, we got the same mother! (*Then suddenly looking at him as MUSIC comes up.*) You know what Reilly . . . I like you!

JERRY. It's Ryan. And I like you too. (*They look at each other for a moment, rise and cross Down Stage. The RESTAURANT disappears and Projections bring us to the fountain at LINCOLN CENTER.*)

GITTEL. You know what my two favorite places are?

JERRY. What?

GITTEL. The fountain in front of the Plaza and the fountain here at Lincoln Center. Hey, look who's conducting tonight, Leonard Bernstein! (GITTEL, *using the chopsticks from the RESTAURANT, begins to conduct. As if from thin air, the Offstage* CHORUS *begins to vocalize. Then* JERRY *tries to conduct, but gets no sound. Finally, with* GITTEL's *help, they get a nice counterpoint "ba-ba" chorus going, and they begin to sing.*)

JERRY.
YOU'RE A CELLO . . . VERY MELLOW!
I'M A DOUBLE BASS BASSOON.

GITTEL.
TWO COMPLETELY UNRELATED INSTRUMENTS
BUT WHEN THEY PLAY TOGETHER
THEY'RE IN TUNE.

JERRY.
DIFF'RENT BACKGROUNDS
DIFF'RENT PARENTS
MILES APART THIS AFTERNOON

GITTEL.
TWO ABSURDLY DIFF'RENT PERSONALITIES
BUT NOW THAT WE'RE TOGETHER
WE'RE IN TUNE!

BOTH.
COLD STRANGERS CAN GET HOT
IT TAKES ONE BOTTLE OF BEER!
A GLOW IS WHAT WE GOT

WE'RE LIT UP LIKE A HUNDRED CANDLE
  CHANDELIER

JERRY.
YOU'RE A SKYLARK!

GITTEL.
I'M A SKYLARK!
YOU'RE A LAZY, CRAZY LOON!

BOTH.
TWO BIRDS OF A DIFF'RENT FEATHER MEET
  ONE NIGHT
SOMEHOW THEY SOUND SO VERY, VERY SWEET
  THAT NIGHT
FOR WHEN THEY SING TOGETHER
THEY'RE IN TUNE!
  (*They conduct a little more, then dance: first a waltz,
  then a polka version of the song. Finishing their dance
  Center Stage, they end the song.*)
TWO BIRDS OF A DIFF'RENT FEATHER MEET
  ONE NIGHT
SOMEHOW THEY SOUND SO VERY VERY SWEET
  THAT NIGHT
FOR WHEN THEY SING TOGETHER
THEY'RE
IN
TUNE!

JERRY. . . . Well, Gittel, I've always heard the best thing
to do with a new friendship is to solidify it.
GITTEL. Solidify it?
JERRY. (*Moving toward her.*) By some word, some deed,
some act . . .
GITTEL. Act, act! Oh my God I almost forgot! Sophie is
acting tonight and I promised to be there!
JERRY. Sophie?
GITTEL. My best girl friend! She's a rock singer but she
wants to be a Shakespearean actress. Mobile Street Theater!
(*As they hurry off.*) . . . They're doing Hamlet! (*We hear
cheers in distance, and the voices of* ACTORS.) . . . In the
original Puerto Rican! (*They exit Stage Right, and the
MOBILE STREET THEATER WAGON rolls on Stage Left
with* ACTORS *performing the last scene of* Hamlet *in Puerto
Rican.*)

LAERTES. (*Falling.*)
Cai en mi trampa
Osrico, come estupido avecilla
Soy victima de mi propia traicion.

SOPHIE. (*As* GERTRUDE, *drinking from poisoned cup, making the most of it.*) Querido, Hamlet! El vino, el vino! (*Lots of choking, gasping.*) . . . Muero envenenada! (*And with a spectacular fall, grasping at her throat, she dies.*)

HAMLET. Oh, vileza! Cerrad todas las puertas Traicion! Traicion! Buscad donde es oculta!

GITTEL. (*Entering with* JERRY *Stage Right, speaking over the Spanish "Hamlet" dialogue.*) Oh my God, she's dead already. We missed it.

JERRY. Which one is she?

GITTEL. That one over there, the big lump on the floor. Whatever you do, don't tell her. It will really kill her.

LAERTES. (*Continuing with dialogue.*) Aqui esta, Hamlet. Tu vas a morir! Esta en tu mano el traidor instrumento con punta y emponzonada. Mi ardid volviose contra mi. Mirame, caido para siempre, tu madre envenenada . . . No puedo mas! El Rey, El Rey es el culpable! (HAMLET *starts for* KING.)

HAMLET.
La punta enponzonada
Veneno, haz tu oficio! (*Stabbing* KING, *then dying himself.*) Siento le muerte, Horacio. Ya el veneno con su potencia doblega me espiritu; no podre oir las nuevas de Fortinbras. Diselo, y todo lo que aqui ha habido: Lo indigno y lo grande. El resto es silencio. (*He dies, the Play ends. The* SPECTATORS *applaud the bowing "HAMLET"* CAST. *The curtain closes on the MOBILE STREET THEATER WAGON. Excited* SPECTATORS, *who had been facing Up Stage watching the Play, turn Downstage with exclamations.*)

SPECTATORS.
Que buena!
Todos great!
La plaquita es terifico!
Ai, papi, what a Hamlet!

JERRY. What is that . . . Spanish? English?

GITTEL. Neither and both. The two of them put together. Spanglish!

(*MUSIC has come up through this.* JULIO GONZALES *turns and begins singing to* GITTEL, JERRY, *and then to* SOPHIE, *who runs from behind the* WAGON *and joins them.*)

JULIO.
BUENOS AMIGO . . . 'ALLO!
MAMMA . . . 'ALLO!
POPPA . . . 'ALLO!
ANGLISH IS WHAT WE DON' KNOW
POPPA DON' KNOW
MOMMA DON' KNOW
SPANGLISH IS LANGLISH WE KNOW
SPANGLISH IS EXPRESSIVO!
MUSICA IS TIPICO
UPTOWN IN EL BARRIO!

(Two GIRLS *turn to join* JULIO, *singing in close harmony.*)

JULIO and Two GIRLS.
POPPA FROM SAN JUAN, P.R.
HE PLAY GUITAR
DOWN IN P.R.
MAMMA SHE FROM ALCAZAR
MAMMA CANTAR
IN ALCAZAR
EL ROCK AND ROLL, THEY DON' KNOW
MUSIC FOR SOUL, THEY DON' KNOW
COMPRA PISTOLA THEY KNOW
WE LIVE IN EL BARRIO!

(JULIO *teaches* JERRY *some Spanglish.*)

JULIO.
CARAMBA!
JERRY.
CARAMBA.
JULIO.
MI MADRE GO SHOPPING.
JERRY.
FOR WHY SHE GO SHOPPING?
JULIO.
TO BUY NEW VESTIDO.
JERRY.
OH, TO BUY NEW VESTIDO.
JULIO.
HEY, MISTER, YOU KNOW YOU SPEAK
    SPANGLISH?
JERRY.
I SPEAK SPANGLISH . . .
WHAT DO YOU KNOW? . . . SPANGLISH!

JULIO. Magnifico!

JERRY. Muchos gracias. (*The SONG continues.*)

JULIO.
CORN BEEF AND CABBAGE

GITTEL.
OY VEY!

JULIO.
HAMBURG!

SOPHIE.
OY VEY!

JULIO.
HOT DOG!

JERRY.
OKAY!

JULIO.
ARROZ CON POLLO

SOPHIE.
OLE!

JULIO.
TORRA

GITTEL.
OLE!

JULIO.
VINO

JERRY.
OLE!

JULIO.
CHILI CON CARNE . . . SO-SO
HOT CUCHIFRITOS . . . HO! HO!
HUNDRED SIXTEEN STREET WE GO!
THAT WHERE IS EL BARRIO!
BUENOS AMIGOS . . .

JERRY.
'ALLO!

JULIO.
SOPHIE . . .

SOPHIE.
'ALLO!

JULIO.
GITTEL . . .

GITTEL.
'ALLO!

JULIO.
ANGLISH IS WHAT WE DON' KNOW
POPPA DON' KNOW
MOMMA DON' KNOW

ANGLISH IS WHAT WE DON' KNOW
POPPA DON' KNOW
MOMMA DON' KNOW
SPANGLISH IS LANGLISH WE KNOW
SPANGLISH IS EXPRESSIVO!
MUSICA IS TIPICO!
UPTOWN IS EL BARRIO!

(*DANCE.*)

CHORUS.
LA, LA, LA . . .

(*The NUMBER builds to a flashing climax, as lights are flown in and strung by the* DANCERS, *and finally the* FULL COMPANY *is waving handkerchiefs in a frenzy.*)

JULIO.
EL BARRIO, EL BARRIO, EL BARRIO, EL BARRIO
EL BARRIO, EL BARRIO, EL BARRIO, EL BARRIO
   FULL COMPANY.
EL BARRIO
   JULIO.
EL BARRIO
   FULL COMPANY.
EL BARRIO
   JULIO.
EL BARRIO
   FULL COMPANY. (*Shouts.*)
EL BARRIO!

SOPHIE. (*To* GITTEL, *as the rest of the* COMPANY *holds its position.*) . . . Well, all I can say is he is gorgeous. I have seen big numbers but this is a big number . . . Look, if he tries anything, all I can say is *let* him. Let him try and let him succeed. I can't stay to see how things come out because I have a date with the guy who plays King Claudius. Hmm, gorgeous . . . hmmmm, gorgeous!

(*MUSICAL TAG through which MOBILE THEATER glides off Left, accompanied by* FULL COMPANY. *When Stage is clear,* GITTEL'S APARTMENT *comes slowly in Right.* JERRY *and* GITTEL *enter Right Up Stage of APARTMENT, and the MUSIC fades. A long moment, then* GITTEL *says.*)

GITTEL. Well, this is where I live . . . See! There's my name on the bell. Mosca. All by itself. No roommate . . . Would you . . . er . . .

JERRY. Yes.

GITTEL. Let me finish . . . like to come in? . . . Now answer.

JERRY. Yes.

GITTEL. (*Acts surprised.*) Oh, good! (*They cross into APARTMENT.*) Just don't get any funny ideas.

JERRY. Oh, I won't. I promise. I swear!

GITTEL. All right, you don't have to get religious about it . . . Make yourself comfortable. You like it?

JERRY. It's charming.

GITTEL. You're being polite.

JERRY. A little . . . It's not without personality. Just the one room?

GITTEL. What one room? Didn't you see the divider? (*She pulls Divider.*) Now it's two rooms . . . If I get another divider, I'll have four . . . If I hang out the window, I have a terrace.

JERRY. (*Indicating the bed.*) Oh, now this is nice. (*Crossing to bed.*) . . . Six feet long and wide enough for two.

GITTEL. $99.50 Gimbel's on sale. It's a hide-a-bed only at those prices I'm not hiding it. What kinda bed you got?

JERRY. Salvation Army. Twelve bucks.

GITTEL. What happened to the twenty-eight thousand a year?

JERRY. In Omaha. I'm not allowed to attorney in New York. We don't sleep so well these days . . .

GITTEL. We? You got a roommate?

JERRY. Thousands of them, they're called bedbugs.

GITTEL. You got bedbugs? . . . Kerosene. Scrub it on both sides, put it on a clean floor, and whatever runs out, step on.

JERRY. (*Sniffing.*) I smell something.

GITTEL. I burn incense.

JERRY. No, something else . . . Like old cheese.

GITTEL. That's why I burn the incense. I hate throwing things out. New Year's Eve 1963 I opened a bottle of champagne, I still got half the bottle, it looks like the Dead Sea . . . Do you do things like that?

JERRY. No. I don't like loose ends. It's the lawyer in me. If I'm through with something, I get rid of it.

GITTEL. Oh. Well, that's something we have in common. We're completely opposite about the same thing . . . Hey, can I make you something? A cup of coffee, instant? A piece of pie, frozen. How about a nice big . . . (JERRY *grabs her and kisses her.*) You're very tall. A girl could break her neck.

JERRY. We could try it lying down.

GITTEL. Whatever happened to leading up to things?

JERRY. They don't even do that in Nebraska anymore.

GITTEL. Do it in New York, please. We're old fashioned here. (*He lets go of her.*)

JERRY. Sorry. Something came over me. I was wafted away by the scent of old cheese and dead wine. I'm funny that way.

GITTEL. I'll tell you what way to get funny. It's my house.

JERRY. Okay . . . (*Looks at photo on wall.*) Who's this?

GITTEL. That's me. I'm dancing . . . The graceful, feminine one is my partner, David.

JERRY. Attractive, but *nothing* compared to you.

GITTEL. Don't let *him* hear you say that . . . Listen, he's very talented. Choreographs, too . . . except we can't get anybody important to come see us . . . We were going to rent the theater last year, I saved the money for the rental, three hundred bucks, but I spent it on my ulcer. Two hundred forty bucks for my hemmorhage, sixty bucks on tips. When it comes to saving my life, I'm very grateful.

JERRY. But you're in good shape now?

GITTEL. Oh, thanks, I'm glad you finally noticed . . . (*Moves closer.*) Listen . . . it's er . . . okay if you wanna get funny now. (*He takes her and kisses her . . . longer than she bargained for. She breaks away, breathless.*) I said funny, not hysterical . . . hey, wait a minute . . . how many arms you got? I shouldn't have let you eat that octopus. (*She moves away from him.*) Let's change the subject. You got any diseases I should know about?

JERRY. (*He rises and crosses to her.*) Nothing except my Navy injuries. I was wounded seven times.

GITTEL. Wow! Where?

JERRY. On my head. I keep banging into pipes.

GITTEL. Yeah, you're the tallest guy I ever went out with. My last two boyfriends on *top* of each other were shorter than you.

JERRY. (*Moves to her again.*) This time *I'll* bend.

GITTEL. . . . Will you slow down, I don't even know anything about you. Like what do you like to do?

JERRY. I'll show you.

GITTEL. I mean during the day.

JERRY. Same thing only I pull down the shades . . . (*They kiss, then break.*)

GITTEL. Boy, how long you been on the wagon?

JERRY. A year. (*He starts for her again, she backs away.*)

GITTEL. . . . Look, let's not get all worked up if we're not going to finish it, huh?

JERRY. Who's not going to, huh?

GITTEL. Me, huh! I mean I like you but I got an iron-clad rule. I wouldn't sleep with God Almighty on the first date. What do you want me to be, promiscuous? Give me one good reason why I should . . .

JERRY. Because I don't talk to anybody. I live in a rat hole on West 97th. I've worn out a pair of shoes in the museums and a pair of pants in bad movies . . . And if I hike over one more beautiful bridge by myself so help me I'll jump off! And I don't feel like jumping today because it happens to be my birthday, and besides I don't have clean underwear and I wouldn't want my mother to be ashamed.

GITTEL. (*Taken aback by his outburst.*) Well my God why didn't you say it was your birthday? I mean my God that changes everything! (*MUSIC comes up and* GITTEL *sings.*)

HERE'S HELLO FROM YOUR FRIENDLY
    RECEPTIONIST
WELCOME TO HOLIDAY INN!
DO YOU NEED A BROAD OR A GOOD
    PSYCHOANALYST?
MAYBE A TONIC AND GIN
THERE'S NO GIDEON BIBLE NEXT TO THE BED
COULD YOU READ THE YELLOW PAGES INSTEAD?
HERE IS A KISS FROM YOUR FRIENDLY
    RECEPTIONIST
WELCOME TO HOLIDAY INN!

IS THE MATTRESS TO YOUR LIKING?
IS THE BLANKET NICE AND WARM?
YOU CAN FIND THE SOAP AND TOWELS IN THE
    JOHN?
SO YOU'RE RESTLESS MISTER RYAN
AND YOU NEED A HELPING HAND
FOR A QUARTER TURN THE "MAGIC FINGERS"
    ON.
ALL THROUGH THE NIGHT THERE'S A
    FRIENDLY RECEPTIONIST
EAGER AND READY TO PLEASE
IF YOU'RE IN NEED OF SOME EXTRA ACTIVITY
THERE ARE NO CHARGES OR FEES!
DON'T BE EMBARRASSED AND DON'T BE
    AFRAID
WE'RE USED TO GIVING OUT TRAVELLERS' AID

SO HERE IS A HUG FROM YOUR HORNY
RECEPTIONIST
WELCOME TO HOLIDAY INN!

IF YOU WANT A CUP OF COFFEE
IF YOU WANT A PIECE OF DANISH
I'LL BE READY, I'LL BE WAITING IN THE HALL
AND REGARDLESS OF THE HOUR
SHOULD YOU NEED A WAKE-UP CALL
CALL . . . CALL . . . CALL!

WE HAVE PEOPLE GOING IN AND OUT
YOU KNOW WHAT I MEAN
BUT YOU'RE THE GREATEST LOOKING
TRANSIENT
I'VE EVER SEEN!
SO HERE'S A HELLO FROM YOUR SEXY
RECEPTIONIST
ONE BIG HELLO FROM YOUR RED HOT
RECEPTIONIST

. . . "HAPPY BIRTHDAY TO YOU?" . . .
WELCOME
TO HOLIDAY INN!

(*Blackout.* GITTEL *exits Right.* JERRY *takes off his shirt and gets into the bed. Projections show us it is morning, as the lights come up again on* GITTEL'S APARTMENT. JERRY *is still asleep as* GITTEL *enters Right with a toothbrush. She crosses to the kitchen, gets a cup of coffee, drinks a little, and puts the cup on the bed table for* JERRY. *As she turns away from the bed,* JERRY *wakes.*)

JERRY. Good morning, Miss Mosca.
GITTEL. Thank God, he remembered my name. Hey, you hungry?
JERRY. I'm starved.
GITTEL. I got something to tell you.
JERRY. What?
GITTEL. I can't cook.
JERRY. I have something to tell you.
GITTEL. What?
JERRY. I have a wife.
GITTEL. I like my news better.
JERRY. That is, I had a wife. I mean she's divorcing me.

GITTEL. (*Crossing to the bed.*) What is she . . . crazy? Was she in a bad mood or something?

JERRY. The pants in the family were being worn by her and her father . . . one in each leg. He took me into the firm, made me a partner, bought me a sixty thousand dollar love nest, which happened to be right next to his. A marriage tends to get a little shaky when the husband has to keep saying "Thank you" each day.

GITTEL. So how do you feel? About the breakup, I mean?

JERRY. I felt bad. Now I'm not so sure how I feel. Something like taking a cold tablet . . . just sitting around waiting for it to go to work.

GITTEL. And I'm the cold tablet, right? Never mind. (*They kiss. A long moment, then.*) Jerry, we can't. I got a ballet class.

JERRY. That's okay, I've got things to do, too. There's a lawyer in this town I went to school with, Paul Bates . . . and I'm going to ask him if there's anything in his office for a thirty-six-year-old legal genius who's never taken the New York Bar! Gittel, I suddenly feel like being a breadwinner!

GITTEL. Good. . . . I suddenly feel like being a bread . . . Speaking of bread, I know you're a little short, moneywise, I mean. Do you know who could fix up your rat hole for practically nothing? David. He's got wonderful ideas about decorating. You should see his place, just like Bendel's window! Only one thing, he's gay, so no cracks . . . You know what it is, gay?

JERRY. Happy?

GITTEL. Yeah, he's happy!

JERRY. Oh, I think I've heard the word before, young lady.

GITTEL. Listen, they got a lot of problems. I'll take you on the next march in Central Park, you hear a few speeches, you're ready to fight.

JERRY. When do unmarried Jewish girls with ulcers march?

GITTEL. They can't: the park's not big enough to hold them. So whadda' ya say, s'okay about David?

JERRY. Sure, go ahead.

GITTEL. Say it again.

JERRY. Sure, go ahead.

GITTEL. Nah, you know what I mean.

JERRY. Local colloquialism.

GITTEL. Oh, what the hell, so I miss one ballet class.

(GITTEL *crosses to the bed, jumps on it, and there is a Blackout during which* GITTEL'S APARTMENT *is winched off. The projection screens rise, the STUDIO mirror flies in*

and the BALLET TRANSITION begins. DAVID *and the*
DANCE COMPANY *enter Stage Right doing ballet com-*
binations. At a point in the transition, the STUDIO mirror
flies out, the Projections change to JERRY'S *neighborhood,*
and JERRY'S APARTMENT *is slowly moved on Right.* GITTEL
is in the APARTMENT getting ready to serve dinner.
DAVID *enters.*)

DAVID. I've got it. We'll bring on the three girls from stage
left doing that kick routine, only reversed.

GITTEL. I don't know what you're talking about but I love
it! (JERRY *enters.*)

DAVID. Hi Jerome.

GITTEL. (*She rushes to him. They kiss.*) Hiya honey.

JERRY. Hey, that looks great! Things are really starting to
shape up here.

DAVID. What's to decorating?

GITTEL. (*She gets wine from under sink.*) 8.95 to decorate
the whole thing so far including the wine. (*Putting the cas-*
serole on picnic cloth on floor, handing wine to DAVID.) A
Beaujolais, imported, and the man at the store said 1970 was
a very good year for Guatemala.

JERRY. (*Sniffing casserole.*) This smells terrific! What is it?

DAVID. I have no idea, I just cook it. (*Bringing his plate*
to the table and sitting.) Now let's all take our time eating . . .

GITTEL and JERRY. (*Finishing it with him.*) . . . it took a
long time to prepare!

JERRY. Your mother say that too?

DAVID. No, my father. Which is why I'm in a little bit of
trouble today.

JERRY. How's the concert going?

DAVID. It's not a concert, it's a showcase . . . go talk to
foreigners.

JERRY. (*Italian.*) Excusa me. I'm-a sorry, what's a showcase?

DAVID. A showcase is when you want to show your talent to
a producer who will make you rich and famous and adored.
But you can't show your talent unless you have a theater
to show your case. But you can't get a theater unless you
give the fink theater owner three hundred dollars for the
night, which we don't have. Which means I'm never going to
become rich, famous and adored! Capisch?

JERRY. Capisch. Hey, how about letting me help?

GITTEL. Look who wants to help . . . Man who makes local
calls collect.

JERRY. Ah but all that's changing! Didn't want to tell you 'till I was sure but there's a possibility of my being admitted to the New York Bar on motion, if Paul Bates sponsors me and I can get my father-in-law to come through with a few affidavits . . . It's one last handout, I know, but once I start practicing you can rent a theater for a year! Well, a small theater.

DAVID. Don't exaggerate, Jerome, after all how much does a lawyer make, I mean it's not like you're a plumber.

GITTEL. And this Paul Bates fellow, how do you know he'll sponsor you?

JERRY. Well, he's given me some briefs to work on and if he likes my work and I have clean fingernails, I'm in. But Miss Mosca, you've got to help me out with him.

GITTEL. Just tell me what you want me to do.

JERRY. He'd just like to get to know me outside of office hours. We're invited to dinner at his place next Friday night.

GITTEL. (*A note of alarm.*) His place? Jerry, where does he live?

JERRY. I've got the address, East 63rd somewhere . . .

GITTEL. OhmyGod! Uptown! That's *dinner.* Jerry, I can't go, I don't fit in there, I got a nosebleed north of 14th Street. (*The telephone rings,* JERRY *goes to answer it.*)

DAVID. Gittel, it's dinner, not the electric chair!

JERRY. (*On phone.*) Hello?

GITTEL. I wish it was, at least there you sit nice, you don't have to think about which fork to use . . .

JERRY. (*On phone.*) I see. Well—would you tell your party Mr. Ryan isn't in at the moment.

GITTEL. (*Hissing.*) What not in at the moment, you're right here!

JERRY. (*On phone.*) Operator 365. Thank you. (*He hangs up.*)

GITTEL. Jerry, an operator number, that's long distance. How do you know it isn't somebody sick or something?

JERRY. It was Omaha, Gittel! The soon-to-be-ex-Mrs. Ryan and I'm not up to that tonight.

DAVID. My God, the souvlaki, it's still in the oven! (*He rushes to the oven, returning with blackened pan, looks at* GITTEL *and* JERRY.) Tragedy. Greek tragedy. (*Starting to exit.*) Don't worry, we'll eat.

GITTEL. Where are you going?

DAVID. Outside to beg for food. (*He exits.*)

GITTEL. (*Rushing into* JERRY's *arms and kissing him.*) Excuse me for being so happy, but I've got a good reason.

JERRY. What?

GITTEL. I'm very happy you're gonna become a regular New York lawyer, David's going to get his theater and become adored and I'm right where I want to be. (*She pulls his arms tighter.*) I wonder why everything's suddenly gonna fall apart.

JERRY. Why do you say that?

GITTEL. Because it's what always happens. That's what Gittel means in Jewish. Things will fall apart.

JERRY. You know what you are? You're lovable.

GITTEL. What I am is a lunatic.

JERRY. (*He sings.*)
YOU'RE A LOVABLE LUNATIC
AN IMPOSSIBLE CASE
BUT I'M QUEER FOR LUNATICS
'SPECIALLY A LUNATIC
WITH A LOVABLE FACE!

AN INCREDIBLE MANIAC
YOU'RE SO FIERCELY INTENSE
BUT WHATEVER YOU DO
IS SO RIGHT AND SO TRUE
THAT SOMEHOW IT MAKES SENSE

IN YOUR INSANELY GENEROUS WAY
YOU GAVE MY WORLD A LIFT
WHAT I MEAN TO SAY IS:
YOU'RE A VERY SPECIAL GIFT

YOU'RE A FUNNY PHENOMENON
AND I LOVE WHAT YOU DO
THOUGH YOU ARE OUT OF YOUR MIND
I'M SO LUCKY TO FIND
A LOVABLE LUNATIC . . . LIKE YOU

WITH EVERY CRAZY THING YOU SAY
YOU MAKE ME LAUGH AND SMILE
YOU ARE WARM, YOU'RE VERY SWEET
I'D LIKE TO STAY A WHILE

SO I'M CHANGING MY ALPHABET
NOW IT STARTS WITH A "U"
I'M SO GLAD YOU'RE AROUND
I'M SO GLAD I HAVE FOUND
A LOVABLE LUNATIC . . .
GUESS WHO?

(*Telephone rings.*)

GITTEL. Aren't you going to answer it?
JERRY. It's not important. (*Telephone rings again.*)
GITTEL. It sounds important to me. (JERRY *goes to phone,
picks it up.*)
JERRY. Hello. Hello, Tess. No, I didn't want to talk to you
the other times. I'm doing it now by special request. What's
that, woman's intuition? Yes, she is. Her name's Gittel. I do,
very much. Tess, are you calling me halfway across the con-
tinent to talk about the furniture? Why don't you burn it . . .
we'll split the insurance. Actually I thought you were calling
to ask me to represent you in the divorce. Of course I have no
intention of contesting it. Tell your father he can file anytime.
What? If I need money I can earn it. I have a job, a girl,
an apartment, it all adds up to a life, a beginning. No I'm not
interested in being friends. Tess, don't . . . please . . . please
don't. Tess . . . (*And he hangs up the phone. A pause.*)
GITTEL. Her cold tablet doesn't seem to be working.
JERRY. Gittel, turn around. Look at me. Don't pretend. It
hurts . . . show me that it hurts.
GITTEL. It hurts.
JERRY. Give me something to hold on to, Gittel. Need me.

(*There is a momentary pause, then* GITTEL *rushes into* JERRY'S
arms. They kiss, a beat, then JERRY'S APARTMENT *glides
off. They exit Up Stage Right as* GITTEL'S APARTMENT
comes on Stage Left with DAVID *on the Telephone.*)

DAVID. No, Sophie, I can't let you talk to her. Tonight's
the big dinner with Jerome uptown. She's been in the john
for the past half hour. She's done her makeup three times . . .
the last time I sent her back she had eyebrows like Theda
Bara, lips like Clara Bow, and I don't know how she did it
but her nose looked like Barbra Streisand. She's had on
everything she owns, including her prom dress . . . don't
laugh, it's the one I like best . . . where are you? At the
club? So who's there? *Oh!* They do what dance? They do
what? They do? They *don't! That* dirty? Listen, Sophie, I'll
be there as soon as I can get her together. Sophie, I can't talk
anymore, I'm trying to get through to Jerome to tell him she's
gonna be late. Okay . . . bye. (DAVID *hangs up, then dials
again.*) Hello, operator, remember me? Yeah, Mr. Ryan's extension please . . . Okay, thanks . . . (*He hangs up, then to*

GITTEL, *who has been fumbling through dresses piled on her bed.*) His line's still busy, Git.

GITTEL. Oh, God, he hates it when I'm late and tonight of all nights.

DAVID. You finished?

GITTEL. *Fisnished* is the only word. He'll hate it . . . even if it fit what'll I do about the spot? I got it . . . lighter fluid. (*She gets lighter fluid from bed table, pours it on dress she is wearing and rubs.*)

DAVID. Wonderful . . . now the spot's out but if somebody lights a cigarette near you . . . shish kebob.

GITTEL. (*She gets green dress from bed, holds it up in front of her.*) How about this?

DAVID. That one's not too bad . . . it's . . . better.

GITTEL. One look and they'll send me around to the service entrance. They'll think I'm from Gristede's. Try Jerry again . . . I'll wear the red, it only clashes with the boa. Besides, it's long enough to hide the shoes which don't go with the cape. (*She puts on red dress with great trouble, and it is horrible.*)

DAVID. (*Redialing.*) Hi, it's me again . . . Yeah, Mr. Ryan's extension, please. Okay . . . thanks. (*He hangs up.*)

GITTEL. Oh my God, David, it's not even the clothes, it's me. I don't belong with those people, they're gonna laugh at me. Maybe I'll stay at home and just send the dress.

DAVID. You know what you've got an overabundance of . . . lack of confidence.

GITTEL. You're right, you're right. Stop it. Stop it right now, Gittel Mosca, you happen to be a very beautiful sophisticated young woman, dressed in the height of fashion, if only it were 1932 on a rainy night in the middle of the Depression . . . I'm not going. (*She takes the red dress off.*)

DAVID. Don't start that again. You have to go. Now what are you going to wear?

GITTEL. (*Getting pants suit from closet.*) The pants suit. It's refined because it's black, and it's sophisticated too 'cause it reveals just a hint of the belly button. (*Holds up pants suit with huge cut-out over the stomach.*) . . . David, call him again, it's an office, tell her to interrupt, I've got to get through to him . . . say it's an emergency. (*As DAVID dials the number again, GITTEL suddenly gets an ulcer attack, but doesn't let him know. She sits on the bed and listens to his telephone conversation.*)

DAVID. Hi! It's me again . . . could you interrupt, it's an emergency. Well, long distance from how long, 'cause if it's only from Newark or somewhere like that you can break in

. . . oh . . . Omaha, well that's long distance . . . okay, thanks. (*He hangs up.*) Probably business . . .

GITTEL. Yeah . . . oh what the hell, I'll wear the green . . . uneven hems are in this year.

DAVID. Oh, listen, Sophie called. She wants us to come to the club. You and Jerome meet me there after dinner . . . You look smashing. You're gonna be terrific. (*He kisses her.*)

GITTEL. I love you. (DAVID *exits Stage Right. The MUSIC underscores* GITTEL'S *pain as she crosses to the kitchen where she gets a bottle of pills. Slowly she crosses back to the sofa, sits, and takes two pills. She makes up her mind to meet* JERRY, *rises, and crosses to the mirror. She pulls herself together and throws on her boa. As the MUSIC swells, she walks out into the street. As* GITTEL'S APARTMENT *glides off Left, the projection screens rise, and the Projections show us a blue Codalith of New York City. She sings.*)

HE'S GOOD FOR ME!
BUT AM I GOOD FOR HIM?
GOOD ENOUGH FOR HIM?
HOW CAN I IMPRESS HIS FRIENDS
STAND .THERE LIKE A DOPE
AND "YES" HIS FRIENDS
I'D BE OUT OF PLACE . . . I'M WRONG
HE WOULD SEE I DON'T BELONG
HE WOULD TRY TO BUILD ME UP
LIKE A POOR, UNWANTED PUP.

I KNOW HE'S GOOD FOR ME
BUT AM I GOOD FOR HIM?
GOOD ENOUGH FOR HIM?
I CAN'T SEE THE LIKES OF HIM
SETT'LING FOR THE LIKES OF ME
NOW FROM WHERE I'M SITTING
MY LOVE LIFE LOOKS HOPELESSLY GRIM
SO WHY DO I KEEP KIDDING MYSELF
I'M NOT SMART ENOUGH
I'M NOT FINE ENOUGH
I'M NOT SWELL ENOUGH
SURE! SO HE'S GOOD FOR ME
BUT I'M NOT GOOD ENOUGH FOR HIM.

(*At the end of the SONG,* GITTEL *stands Center Stage, and the BANANA CLUB is brought on around her. Tables and chairs, a band stand, and a huge neon banana are flown and winched in. The* DANCERS *are doing a slow*

motion version of a new dance called "The Ride." At a
Table Center sit DAVID, OSCAR *and* SOPHIE.)

DAVID. Hello Mrs. Jerome, a little early aren't you? Where's
Mr. Jerome?

GITTEL. Get me a drink, David.

DAVID. You want a drink?

GITTEL. *I want a drink.*

OSCAR. Gittel, I didn't know you were going to be here
tonight.

GITTEL. Oscar, that makes two of us.

SOPHIE. Honey, where's Jerry?

GITTEL. Why is everybody so concerned about Jerry?

SOPHIE. You didn't have a fight, did you?

GITTEL. I haven't even seen him. I never got as far as East
63rd.

DAVID. What stopped you?

GITTEL. East 62nd.

DAVID. Fun-n-n-ny! (WAITER *comes up to the Table.*) A
Double Scotch, a rum and coke and a screwdriver . . .

GITTEL. . . . and I'll have the same.

SOPHIE. Git, what are you doing to yourself . . . your
ulcer . . .

GITTEL. Why is everybody always talking about my ulcer?
I got no other charms? (*She reaches for a cigarette.*)

DAVID. Oh no, you're charming . . . *charming!*

OSCAR. You know, I've really missed you.

GITTEL. Listen Oscar, we had a nice affair once, and believe
me it was the best five minutes I ever spent . . . but I
wouldn't want to infringe on the memory of it to ever let it
happen again.

(*MUSIC starts and projection screens rise.* SPARKLE *and* THE
SPARKLETTES *are revealed on the Band Stand.*)

SPARKLETTES.
DO THE RIDE, DO THE RIDE, DO IT CHILDREN
DO THE RIDE, DO THE RIDE

SPARKLE. (*From Band Stand.*) Hey Sophie, get on up here!
(SOPHIE *leaves the Center Table and crosses to the Band
Stand.*)

SPARKLETTES.
DO THE RIDE, DO THE RIDE, DO IT CHILDREN
DO THE RIDE, DO THE RIDE

SOPHIE.
RIDE

CHORUS. (*On Stage, the* PATRONS *of the CLUB.*)
R . . . I . . . D . . . E . . . RIDE!

SPARKLE.
RIDE OUT THE STORM
RIDE OUT THE STORM
HOPE IS YOUR LIFEBELT
COME ON, RIDE OUT THE STORM
IN THIS COLD SEA OF TROUBLE
WE'LL BE SAFE, WE'LL BE WARM
IF WE ALL PULL
  TOGETHER
WHILE WE RIDE OUT
  THE. . . .

SPARKLETTES.
WHILE WE RIDE
WHILE WE RIDE
WHILE WE RIDE
WHILE WE RIDE
OUT THE STORM

RIDE OUT THE STORM
IF YOU DON'T
LIKE YOUR
  NEIGHBORS
JUST THE WAY THEY
  DON'T LIKE YOU
I SAY FRIENDS
LIKE YOUR
  NEIGHBORS
WHAT THE HELL IS
  THERE TO DO?
RELAX AND
RIDE OUT THE STORM
RIDE OUT THE STORM
FASTEN YOUR SEAT
  BELT
C'MON RIDE

DON'T
LIKE YOUR
  NEIGHBORS

FRIENDS
LIKE YOUR
  NEIGHBORS
HELL IS THERE TO
  DO?

OO-OO-OO-OO-OO-OO

CHORUS.
C'MON RIDE, C'MON
  RIDE
C'MON RIDE, C'MON
  RIDE
C'MON RIDE. . . .

RIDE OUT THE STORM!

CHORUS.
DO THE RIDE, DO THE RIDE, DO IT CHILDREN
DO THE RIDE, DO THE RIDE! (*Vamp.*)

(DANCERS *begin a frenzied highly suggestive dance, as* DAVID
gapes in amazement, then finally joins in.)

DAVID. Oh my God! (*DANCE continues, then . . .*)

CHORUS.
R . . . I . . D . . . E . . .
RIDE IT, RIDE IT
RIDE IT, RIDE IT
RIDE IT, RIDE IT, RIDE IT, RIDE IT
DO THE RIDE, DO THE RIDE, DO IT CHILDREN
DO THE RIDE, DO THE RIDE, DO IT CHILDREN
DO THE RIDE, DO THE RIDE, DO IT CHILDREN
DO THE RIDE, DO THE RIDE, DO IT CHILDREN

SOPHIE.
YOU RIDE WITH ME
AND I'LL RIDE WITH YOU
AND I'LL SHOW YOU JUST HOW EASY
THE RIDE IS TO DO

CHORUS.
DO THE RIDE

SOPHIE.
CHILDREN
RIDE OUT THE STORM
RIDE OUT THE STORM
FAITH IS YOUR ANCHOR
WHEN YOU RIDE OUT THE STORM
STICK TO WHAT YOU BELIEVE IN
DON'T RETRACT . . . DON'T REFORM
IF IT'S LOVE YOU BELIEVE IN
YOU WILL RIDE, RIDE
OUT THE STORM.

SOPHIE.	CHORUS and SPARKLETTES.
WHEN THE SKY	WHEN THE SKY
STARTS TO DARKEN	IT GOES BLACK
DON'T YOU GO AND	
BLOW YOUR STACK	

FULL COMPANY.
WHEN THE SEA DOGS START BARKIN'

SOPHIE.
AIN'T NO SENSE IN
   BARKIN' BACK
BE PATIENT   CHORUS.
RIDE OUT THE STORM   RIDE IT OUT, RIDE IT
                                   OUT

SOPHIE.
RIDE OUT THE STORM
FASTEN YOUR SEAT
  BELT
C'MON RIDE

RIDE OUT THE STORM.

FULL COMPANY.
RIDE, RIDE, RIDE, RIDE, RIDE, RIDE,
RIDE, RIDE
RIDE OUT THE STORM

CHORUS.
C'MON RIDE OUT THE
STORM

C'MON RIDE, C'MON
  RIDE
C'MON RIDE, C'MON
  RIDE

SPARKLETTES.
DO THE RIDE
  CHILDREN
DO THE RIDE
  CHILDREN
DO THE RIDE
  CHILDREN

RIDE!

(*Musical Tag as the* FULL COMPANY *and the BANANA CLUB
  clear the Stage. Projections show us late night in* GITTEL'S
  neighborhood. GITTEL'S APARTMENT *glides in Stage Left
  with* GITTEL, *obviously in great pain, on the Telephone.
  She is doubled over on the Sofa.*)

GITTEL. Dr. Seegan please . . . No. No, Dr. Seegan. *I'm*
calling, who are you, I mean are you real or still that answer-
ing thing . . . Look, just get him for me . . . Yeah . . . It's
an emergency . . . tell him it's happening again. It's a half
hour since I took the pills and they're not working . . . well
I don't care, just find him . . . somewhere . . . please, now
. . . yeah, thanks . . . (*With great effort, she hangs up the
phone and slowly makes her way to the bed. With the pillow
clutched to her stomach she lies down on the bed.* JERRY *enters
Stage Right, standing silently and looking at* GITTEL.) Oh,
hiya Jerry, how was your dinner . . . have a good time?
  JERRY. I waited in that lobby for a goddam hour-and-a-
half. What the hell happened to you?
  GITTEL. I don't know . . . I, I lost the address, then I . . .
I met some friends and had a couple of drinks and that's why
I forgot to come uptown. Jerry, it's late and I gotta get some
sleep.

JERRY. Gittel, let's get this over with. What were you doing at Oscar's place?

GITTEL. Who said I was at Oscar's?

JERRY. I finally got Sophie at midnight. She said you'd been at the Club and left with Oscar. Well, how was it?

GITTEL. How was what? My God, I had a few drinks, I didn't feel like being alone so I had a nightcap with Oscar.

JERRY. 'Til now? I don't buy that.

GITTEL. Look, we both know I'm dumb so if you want to ask something ask it as least so a normal dumb person could understand.

JERRY. If that's the way you want it, did he lay you, did he ball you . . .

GITTEL. (*A shout.*) So what if he did! That's the end of the world?

JERRY. Gittel, what are you doing to us? (*And* JERRY *suddenly shakes her hard.* GITTEL *falls back and the bottle of pills flies from her hand.* JERRY *picks them up and sees what they are.*) When did the pain start?

GITTEL. When you came in! And it'll go when you do. (*Telephone rings through last of this.* GITTEL *glances at it with sharp nervousness, knowing who it is.*) . . . So go, please, willya?

JERRY. Aren't you going to answer it?

GITTEL. Not now.

JERRY. Who's it calling this late, him?

GITTEL. How the hell should I know, maybe it's a wrong number, Sophie . . . look are you gonna just stand there holding those pills, or are you gonna give them to me. (*Telephone stops ringing.*)

JERRY. How many are you supposed to take?

GITTEL. Two. And you better give me two more for my head.

JERRY. Did I hurt you?

GITTEL. Sure you hurt me! What do you think I'm made, out of tin? (*She takes pills.*) All right, you wanna know? I went with Oscar because I belong with Oscar! I know him since I was a kid; we used to neck in hallways. He's penny candy, Oscar. I pay a penny, I get a penny's worth. But you, you're some big ten buck box of Barricini . . . Look at me! Am I what East 63rd expects you to be with? Her, from Omaha, who you were on the phone with all afternoon . . . That's what they expect and that's what I'll never be! And I can't change, Jerry! Like Wally, my last boyfriend, he wanted me to get braces on my teeth only I said face it, I got two teeth a little buck, you gotta take me the way I am! And we both know what I am, Jerry . . . Nothing.

JERRY. Gittel, you're something very special, and you're the only one who doesn't know it . . . I'm going. And I love your two teeth a little buck.

GITTEL. Jerry! Don't go! . . . the only thing I did in Oscar's was faint in the john . . . That's when I found I . . . I'm bleeding, Jerry!

JERRY. (*Wheeling.*) What?

GITTEL. I'm bleeding, Jerry . . . And I'm so scared this time.

JERRY. Gittel! (*Running to her, taking her by arm to bed.*) . . . Who's your doctor?

GITTEL. Seegan. That musta been him on the phone. But you'd better call the hospital . . . St. Vincent's . . . that's where I was last time.

JERRY. (*Grabbing phone book, tearing open pages.*) You lunatic, you God damn nitwit, why didn't you tell me?

GITTEL. I didn't want to trap you, Jerry . . .

JERRY. Trap me?

GITTEL. Into staying with me. I hate myself, but I can't help it! I don't want you to leave me, Jerry.

JERRY. (*Holding her, dialing with free hand.*) I'm not leaving, I'm here! (*As* GITTEL *clutches his hand saying* "It hurts, Jerry . . . Jerry I love you . . . It hurts, Jerry . . . I love you.") . . . St. Vincent's? Can you send an ambulance right away? *Now,* it's an *emergency!* 342 East Fourth, right away . . . right away . . . (*By now Curtain is down.*)

END OF ACT ONE

ACT TWO

ENTR'ACTE

As the CURTAIN rises, we see two HOSPITAL beds. In the bed Stage Left is ETHEL with her leg in traction, and GITTEL is in the Stage Right bed.

There is a screen on each bed which conceals ETHEL and GITTEL, as well as the SINGERS and DANCERS who are ready to burst forth from HOSPITAL room as soon as the NURSE says . . .

NURSE. Eight o'clock . . . all visitors must leave . . . please!

(The two screens are pushed apart, and all the VISITORS rush out with champagne bottles, flowers, candy, etc., and exit Stages Right and Left, followed by the NURSE. GITTEL'S and ETHEL'S beds are now open to the audience. JERRY enters right and crosses first to GITTEL, then to ETHEL.)

JERRY. Hi, honey, sorry I'm late . . . had to duck through maternity to get in. Ethel, how you doing?

ETHEL. The better for seeing you, beautiful. Hey, what's in the bag? No, don't tell me!

JERRY. *(Handing it to her.)* Number Three Stage Special, just what you ordered. See if I got it right.

ETHEL. *(Taking huge sandwich out of bag.)* Corned-beef, hot pastrami, turkey white meat only, imported swiss, lettuce, tomato, hard-boiled egg and chopped liver . . . on raisin bread! There's only one way to show my gratitude. Have your way with me! I'm all set up for it . . . On second thought I better eat first to get up my strength. *(As JERRY pulls rolling screen around her bed.)* Oh my God, there's cole slaw, too. And do I spy a little pickle . . . I do!

JERRY. There's no need for those hurt eyes, Miss Mosca . . . I brought you something too. A gift. Had to go to twelve different stores to find it! To remind you of the night when first we met.

GITTEL. Oh, Jerry! A tall pink chicken! Just what I always wanted.

JERRY. It's a flamingo, dummy! Well, actually it's a stork, but we dipped it. And not just an ordinary flamingo, my child, a magic one! When things go wrong just rub it thrice, say "You're a beautiful flamingo" twice . . . and everything'll come out nice.

GITTEL. (*Looking.*) It's a boy flamingo or a girl flamingo?

JERRY. What difference does it make?

GITTEL. Where to rub . . . Now I'm not mad 'cause you were late.

JERRY. I have a better excuse than that. Had to stop by the apartment. Paul Bates lent me eight volumes of the Civil Practises Act and I dropped them off on the way . . . (*The News.*) . . . I've decided to learn a few statutes, Gittel.

GITTEL. What for?

JERRY. I called my father-in-law today and told him to shove the affidavits. I suddenly got the idea that if I asked him for this one last favor, there'd be another one last favor lurking behind it. So I'm pitting my aging brain against the New York State Bar Exam . . . (*Before she can interrupt.*) . . . Which happens to fall exactly two weeks after the date of your showcase.

GITTEL. What showcase? What are you talking about?

JERRY. Yours and David's. January 28th. Been doing some extra work at the office and this morning I dropped off three hundred bucks at the theatre.

GITTEL. Oh, Jerry, what did I do to deserve you? Have a hemorrhage. Some girls got a gorgeous shape, I got a sexy ulcer.

JERRY. You sure do!

GITTEL. (*As he starts under covers.*) Jerry please . . . Jerry stop! Not on Blue Cross! (*Indicating screen.*) Besides, this is a semi-private room.

ETHEL. (*From behind screen.*) I can't hear a thing. I'm in a corned-beef coma!

GITTEL. (*Unable to hold it in.*) Jerry, you know what? I love you. I shouldn't say it so much but I can't help it.

JERRY. I'm glad you say it, Gittel.

GITTEL. Still, I'll try not to say it too often. Twice a week! Hey . . . what're you doing? (JERRY *takes blankets down.*)

JERRY. Getting you up. I feel like taking a walk with my girl. Besides, the doctor said if you don't get up today your blood will rust. (*Putting her slippers on.*)

GITTEL. So maybe I like rusty blood.

JERRY. You may, I don't. And two of those pints came from me.

GITTEL. So take 'em back, Indian giver! (*She's up now.*)
. . . Jerry, I'm dizzy!

JERRY. (*Jewish.*) So vat else is new? (*And he sings, while gently walking her around.*)
WE'VE GOT IT
I'M AFRAID WE'VE GOT IT!
THAT LIVELY URGE WHEN WE'RE ALONE
THE FEELING THAT FIRST NIGHT I MET YOU
HAS SIMPLY GROWN AND GROWN AND GROWN
A LUCKY GUY WAS I TO SPOT IT
TO VIEW WHAT LOVE WITH YOU COULD BE
IF YOU ARE FREE, BY CHANCE
MAY I HAVE THIS DANCE?
COMPARED TO YOU THE GALS I'VE KISSED
ARE DULLER THAN A LAUNDRY LIST
BUT BOY WE'VE GOT IT
IT'S WILD, IT'S MAD
AND I'M GLAD.

WE'VE GOT IT
GITTEL GIRL WE'VE GOT IT
WE'VE HIT THE HIGHEST FEVER PITCH
WHAT HAPPENS EVERYTIME I'M NEAR YOU
I ITCH, I ITCH, I ITCH, I ITCH!
WE DIDN'T TRY TO PLAN OR PLOT IT
I'VE NEVER MET A THREAT LIKE YOU
THE DOCTOR SAID "NOW PLEASE
DON'T TOUCH AND DON'T SQUEEZE"
ALTHOUGH MY THOUGHTS ARE SEXUAL
I'LL KEEP THEM INTELLECTUAL
OH HELL WE'VE GOT IT
AND I'M GLAD
(JERRY *starts to dance, a la Fred Astaire.*)
GITTEL. . . . What are you doing?

JERRY. I'm dancing. What does it look like? (*He does a few more steps.*) Don't look so surprised . . . Fred Astaire came from Omaha, ya know! (*The DANCE continues, then . . .*)
WE'VE GOT IT!
I'M AFRAID WE'VE GOT IT!
THAT LIVELY URGE WHEN WE'RE ALONE
THE FEELING THAT FIRST NIGHT I MET YOU
HAS SIMPLY GROWN AND GROWN AND GROWN
A LUCKY GUY WAS I TO SPOT IT
TO VIEW WHAT LOVE WITH YOU COULD BE
I'M NOT SIR GALAHAD
THAT LILY-WHITE LAD

RIGHT NOW MY BLOOD IS HOT FOR YOU
THIS PASSION THAT I'VE GOT FOR YOU
IS LECHEROUS!
AND AM
I
GLAD!

(*End SONG with* GITTEL *and* JERRY *locked in an embrace on
the bed, as the* NURSE, *holding a thermometer, comes into
the room.*)

NURSE. All right ladies . . . time for a little fun and games
. . . (*Seeing* JERRY.) And what sort of therapy is that? (*Cross-
ing to* ETHEL's *bed hidden behind screen.*) No, I don't think
I want to know.

GITTEL. Jerry, I think you'd better go now.

JERRY. So long, Gittel. (*He kisses her.*) See you tomorrow.

GITTEL. See you tomorrow . . . (*Suddenly calling after
him.*) . . . I love you, Jerry! (*Then . . .*) Hell, there goes
the whole week. (JERRY *exits Left, MUSIC begins, and from
her HOSPITAL bed,* GITTEL *sings.*)
POOR EVERYBODY ELSE
HOW I PITY EVERYBODY ELSE BUT ME
I'M SORRY THEY'RE NOT LOVED
LIKE I'M BEING LOVED
IN THIS WORLD THERE'S NO GIRL ALIVE, GOT
THE GOOSE BUMPS THAT I'VE GOT
TODAY
FEEL SO RICH TODAY
I'D GIVE EVERYTHING BUT HIM AWAY
THIS TOWN WOULD FLIP
BUT THEY JUST CAN'T MAKE THE CONTACT
HE'S UNDER EXCLUSIVE CONTRACT TO ME
POOR EVERYBODY ELSE
PITY EVERYBODY ELSE
I COULD SIT DOWN AND CRY FOR
POOR EVERYBODY ELSE BUT ME. . . .

(*The* HOSPITAL ATTENDANTS *enter. They remove and
strike* ETHEL's *bed, and begin to roll* GITTEL's *bed around
the Stage as she sings the second chorus.*)

POOR EVERYBODY ELSE
MY HEART ACHES FOR YOU AND YOU AND
    YOU AND YOU!
WE'RE PHYSICALLY TIED

SPIRITUALLY TIED
LIKE HE SAYS "WE'RE INTERDEPENDERS
LIKE PANTS AND SUSPENDER"
WE MATCH
FUNNY HOW WE MATCH
AND WHAT'S MORE WE HIT IT OFF FROM
   SCRATCH
I LOVE MY FRIENDS
BUT JUST IN CASE THEY ARE TEMPTED
REMEMBER THE GUY'S PRE-EMPTED BY ME
POOR EVERYBODY ELSE
LONELY EVERYBODY ELSE
I COULD SIT DOWN AND CRY FOR
POOR EVERYBODY ELSE BUT
ME!
ME!
ME!

(*The* HOSPITAL ATTENDANTS *roll her off Left, as the DRESS-
ING ROOM OF STUDIO glides on Left.* GITTEL *has just
completed her class, and* JERRY *is with her as she dresses.*)

JERRY. (*Closing law book he has been reading.*) Sure, but
it's ridiculous paying rent on two apartments when you're at
my place all the time!

GITTEL. Are you sure, Jerry? Having my own place is use-
ful. Suppose we have a fight or something . . . I got somewhere to go and be mad! As soon as we finish painting yours,
I'll definitely move in, maybe . . .

JERRY. All right, Gittel, you win. But only because arguing
about who lives where is not what's on my mind right now.
(*He takes her in his arms.*)

GITTEL. Jerry, there's a class going on outside! And besides
you got that statute to learn.

JERRY. It'll wait.

GITTEL. But the Bar Exam won't! Jerry, don't . . . Jerry!
You know that end of my spinal column is one of my highly
erogenous zones . . . (*Moving away from him.*) . . . Besides
we made a deal! One for one! One statute for one moment of
madness!

JERRY. There are over five thousand statutes.

GITTEL. So we got the weekend! (*He is behind her again.*)
. . . Jerry, you have now arrived at an erogenous zone I
didn't even know I had! Quick Jerry, a statute!

JERRY. All right, but I'm picking a raunchy one.

GITTEL. I'm listening, believe me I hear every word . . .

JERRY. Rule 3211. Motion to dismiss a cause of action.

GITTEL. (*Carried away by now.*) Oh yeah, action . . .

JERRY. (*As she repeats key words,* "party, asserted, on the ground," *etc.*) A party may move for judgement dismissing one or more causes of action asserted against him on the ground that . . .

GITTEL. Jerry.

JERRY. Yeah?

GITTEL. This is a long one, hah?

JERRY. Ten clauses.

GITTEL. (*Giving up, into his arms.*) Aah, the hell with it. So you'll be a C.P.A.

(*They embrace, and the Lights go to black for just an instant. As the Lights come up we are in the STUDIO and Projections show us that it is night. The* DANCE COMPANY *is in a freeze behind the STUDIO mirror. We hear during this change* JERRY'S VOICE *[pre-recorded] practicing his law statutes.*)

JERRY'S VOICE. (*Pre-recorded.*) ". . . Article 25, Section 2511, where two or more persons are surety on an undertaking in an action of proceeding they shall be jointly and severally liable in any case involving . . ."

". . . Section 3041, Article 30, any party may require another party to give a bill of particulars of his claim or a copy of the items of the account alleged to be . . ."

". . . Chapter 1, Article 50, Rule 12, the court having ordered a severance may direct judgement upon a cause of action or upon one or more causes of action . . ."

". . . Public Buildings Law, Section 141, Display of Foreign flags on public buildings. It shall not be lawful to display the flags or emblems of any foreign country . . ."

(DAVID *enters Right and joins* JERRY.)

DAVID. I promise you, Jerome . . . if you learn that law stuff in rhythm it will make it a lot easier . . . now say that one again at this tempo: a-one, two, three, four . . . (DAVID *begins tapping to* JERRY'S *recitation.*)

JERRY. (*Spoken in tempo.*)

DUTY!

ON SALT!

DAVID. That's it!

JERRY.
A DUTY OF *ONE* CENT PER BUSHEL OF FIFTY-
SIX *POUNDS*
SHALL BE COLLECTED AND *PAID.* . . .
    DAVID. Wait! (*He executes an intricate step.*) . . . Go!
JERRY.
PAID TO THE TREASURER
    (GITTEL *enters Stage Left.*)
ON *ALL SALT* MANUFACTURED FROM BRINE
FURNISHED BY THE *STATE* FROM THE GREAT
SALT SPRINGS. . . .
    DAVID. (*To* GITTEL.) It fits with that law thing he's learn-
ing.
JERRY.
UPON THE ONONDAGA SALT SPRINGS . . .
RESERVATION!
IN THE COUNTY OF . . .
ONONDAGA!
IN THE STATE OF . . .
NEW YORK!
    DAVID. Watch this one . . . it's new!
    JERRY. (*Plunging in again, still spoken.*)
THE ONONDAGA SALT SPRINGS. . . .
SUPERINTENDENT
MAY ESTABLISH PUBLIC OFFICES
FOR TRANSACTION
OF THE *BUSINESS* CONNECTED
WITH THE *MANUFACTURE*
OF SALT!
    JERRY and DAVID.
SUCH OFFICES. . . .
SHALL BE!
KEPT OPEN EV'RY DAY. . . .
EX-CEPT!
SUNDAYS AND HOLIDAYS
FROM SUNRISE TO SUNSET
AND DURING ANY HOURS
ANY PERSON MAY EXAMINE
ANY ENTRY IN THE LEDGER
THAT THE SUPERINTENDENT KEEPS ON THE
ONONDAGA SALT SPRINGS
RESERVATION!
IN ONONDAGA COUNTY!
IN NEW YORK STATE!
    GITTEL. Terrific . . . hey kids, let's do it from the top.

(MUSIC starts, and the DANCE COMPANY *forms a line, led in a tap number by* DAVID. GITTEL, *distracted by* JERRY, *can't keep in step, and finally begins singing herself.)*

JERRY.
IN THE LATE GREAT STATE OF NEW YORK
IN THE LATE GREAT STATE OF NEW YORK
IN THE COUNTY OF ONONDAGA
IN THE LATE GREAT STATE OF NEW YORK
A DUTY ON SALT, A DUTY OF ONE CENT PER
    BUSHEL OF FIFTY-SIX POUNDS
SHALL BE COLLECTED AND PAID TO THE
    TREASURER
    (He begins to sing.)
ON ALL SALT MANUFACTURED IN THE LATE
    GREAT STATE OF NEW YORK
IN THE LATE GREAT STATE OF NEW YORK
IN THE COUNTY OF ONONDAGA IN THE LATE
    GREAT STATE OF NEW YORK
AND THE STATE COMPTROLLERS
SHALL HEREAFTER HAVE ALL POWERS AND
    DUTIES HERETOFORE CONFERRED ON THE
    FORMER SUPERINTENDENT OF THE
    ONONDAGA COUNTY SALT SPRINGS
NO DEPUTIES, NO INSPECTORS
SHALL BE APPOINTED TO SERVE IN THE
LATE
GREAT
STATE
OF NEW. . . .

GITTEL.	JERRY and CHORUS.
POOR	IN THE LATE GREAT STATE OF NEW YORK
EVERYBODY ELSE	IN THE LATE GREAT STATE OF NEW YORK
HOW I PITY EVERYBODY ELSE	IN THE COUNTY OF ONONDAGA
BUT ME	IN THE LATE GREAT STATE OF NEW YORK
I'M SORRY THEY'RE NOT LOVED	A DUTY OF SALT
LIKE I'M BEING LOVED	A DUTY OF ONE CENT PER BUSHEL OF FIFTY-SIX POUNDS

GITTEL.
IN THIS WORLD
  THERE'S NO GIRL
  ALIVE GOT THE
  GOOSE BUMPS
THAT I'VE GOT TO-
  DAY. . . .

FEEL SO RICH TODAY

I'D GIVE ANYTHING
  BUT HIM
AWAY. . . .

THIS TOWN WOULD
  FLIP
BUT THEY JUST CAN'T
  MAKE THE CONTACT,
  HE'S UNDER
  EXCLUSIVE
  CONTRACT TO
  ME. . . .

POOR EVERYBODY
  ELSE. . . .
LONELY EVERYBODY
  ELSE. . . .
GOT A LUMP IN MY
  THROAT
FOR POOR EVERYBODY
  ELSE BUT. . . .

JERRY and CHORUS.
SHALL BE COLLECTED
  AND PAID TO THE
  TREASURER

ON ALL SALT
  MANUFACTURED
IN THE LATE GREAT
  STATE OF NEW YORK
IN THE LATE GREAT
  STATE OF NEW YORK
IN THE COUNTY OF
  ONONDAGA
IN THE LATE GREAT
  STATE OF NEW YORK
JERRY.
AND THE STATE
  COMPTROLLER
SHALL HEREAFTER
  HAVE ALL POWERS
  AND DUTIES
  HERETOFORE
  CONFERRED ON THE
  FORMER SUPER-
  INTENDENT OF THE
  ONONDAGA SALT
  SPRINGS

NO DEPUTIES, NO
  INSPECTORS
SHALL BE APPOINTED
  TO SERVE

DAVID.
AND-A ONE, TWO, THREE, FOUR. . . .

DANCE COMPANY.
FIVE, SIX, SEVEN, EIGHT. . . .

FULL COMPANY.
GREAT GREAT GREAT
FIRST RATE STATE
ONE TWO THREE FOUR FIVE SIX SEVEN EIGHT
LATE LATE LATE
LATE GREAT STATE

ONE TWO THREE FOUR FIRST RATE STATE
FIVE SIX SEVEN EIGHT LATE GREAT STATE
ONE TWO THREE FOUR FIVE SIX SEVEN EIGHT

GITTEL.	OTHERS.
POOR EVERYBODY ELSE	NO DEPUTIES, NO INSPECTORS
LONELY EVERYBODY ELSE	SHALL BE APPOINTED TO SERVE
GOT A LUMP IN MY THROAT FOR POOR	IN THE
	LATE GREAT STATE OF NEW
EVERYBODY	YORK. . . . IN THE
ELSE	LATE GREAT STATE OF NEW
BUT	YORK
ME	IN THE LATE GREAT STATE OF NEW YORK
ME	IN THE LATE GREAT STATE OF NEW YORK
ME	IN THE LATE GREAT STATE OF NEW YORK
ME!	IN THE LATE GREAT STATE OF NEW YORK

(*BLACKOUT, and the STUDIO is cleared.* JERRY'S APART-
MENT *comes on Stage Right.* GITTEL *enters carrying a
heavy box indicating that she is moving in. She takes an
8X10 glossy picture of herself out of the box and thumb
tacks it to the wall as the Telephone rings.*)

GITTEL. (*Quickly.*) Hello, breadwinner! (*Embarrassed.*)
Oh, I'm sorry . . . I was expecting a call from my baker . . .
Who? . . . Mr. Ryan? . . . No, he's not in yet . . . This is
the girl . . . Who is this? . . . Mrs. Ryan? . . . You mean
Mrs. Ryan? Christ! . . . Yes . . . yes, it is Gittel Mosca . . .
You know about her? . . . Gittel? . . . Yes, a very unusual
name . . . it's of Hebraic origin . . . In Hebrew it means ex-
actly what's happening now . . . Excuse me . . . I've pre-
pared a thousand times what I'd say if we ever had this con-
versation, but you caught me unprepared . . . Listen, has
Jerry told you all about us? . . . Does it bother you? . . .
It doesn't . . . that's very decent of you . . . You get the
feeling we're in a Joan Crawford movie? (*Laughs.*) No, no.
You're Joan Crawford, I'm Ann Blythe . . . Listen, can I say

something very honest to you? . . . I'm very sorry for you
your marriage broke up . . . but I'm very happy for me . . .
Gee, that's a lousy thing for me to say to you . . . I mean
you're even paying long distance charges to hear it . . . New
York? . . . Oh! . . . When did you get in? . . . Well, I
would ask you over but I'll tell you the truth, I don't think
I want to see what you look like . . . My confidence is a little
shaky to begin with, I'd like to picture you ugly if you don't
mind . . . The Gotham Hotel . . . Yes, I'll tell him . . . To
sign what affidavits? . . . The final decree? . . . You mean
you're actually divorced? . . . No, he didn't tell me . . .
(*She is a little shaken by this news.*) But I'm sure he was going
to . . . eventually . . . Some day . . . Well, listen it was very
nice bumping into you like this . . . I want to wish you all
the best of luck in your new life . . . (*Knowing that sounded
wrong.*) Oh God, I'm a real Gittel . . . Goodbye, Mrs. Ryan
. . . (*Just about to hang, an afterthought.*) *Ex*-Mrs. Ryan!
. . . Tess? . . . Oh, okay . . . Tess! (*She hangs up, then
shrugs.*) Look who I just found for a friend! . . . My buddy,
Tess Ryan . . . "Oh, hi Jerry. Why don't ya make yourself a
TV dinner, me and Tess are going to the movies" . . . (*Walks
around, thinking.*) She sounded nice, soft spoken . . . con-
fident . . . educated . . . *dis-gusting!* . . . Looks like the
girl in the Breck Shampoo ad . . . A nice type if you like
1938 . . . Skinny! . . . Tall and skinny! . . . Dina Merrill!
. . . She'll look good when she's eighty . . . Keeps her suntan
in a blizzard . . . No, no . . . Short and squat . . . short
and chunky . . . short and *stacked!* . . . That's it! . . . An
athlete . . . Mrs. Winner . . . (*Through clenched teeth, Vas-
sar.*) "Deddy, Deddy, look, another blue ribbon" . . . Could
beat his pants off in tennis if she wanted . . . but she doesn't
want . . . because she's smart . . . Short, stacked and
smart . . .

JERRY. (*Enters from Left.*) Who's short, stacked and smart?

GITTEL. (*Looks up.*) Napoleon! Will you please stay outa
my thoughts.

JERRY. Then keep them quiet. Do you know you talk to
yourself?

GITTEL. I *like* talking to myself.

JERRY. Why?

GITTEL. When I talk to you, I feel like a jerk. When I talk
to me, I feel like *somebody.* Don't people say "hello" in
Nebraska?

JERRY. (*Hugs her.*) Mr. Ryan is not *in* Nebraska.

GITTEL. (*Pulls away.*) Neither is *Mrs.* Ryan.

JERRY. What do you mean?

GITTEL. She's at the God damn Gotham Hotel . . . She's in the Daddy suite.

JERRY. How do you know?

GITTEL. I just talked to her on the God damned phone. She wants you to sign some God damn affidavits.

JERRY. What are you so mad about?

GITTEL. (*Angrily.*) Because she's *gorgeous!*

JERRY. No, she's not.

GITTEL. Don't tell me. I just talked to the woman. She's gorgeous.

JERRY. She is not gorgeous. She is pretty. She is attractive in a sort of soft, gentle, feminine way.

GITTEL. Oh, Christ, that's worse than gorgeous.

JERRY. How did she sound towards you?

GITTEL. Buddy, buddy. Wednesday I'm going to her place for bridge and Thursday she's coming here for bowling.

JERRY. (*Hugs her again.*) I love it. You're jealous.

GITTEL. I am not jealous. I AM *NOT* JEALOUS . . . You got a picture of her?

JERRY. (*Reaching for his wallet.*) Yes.

GITTEL. (*Quickly.*) I don't want to see it . . . Anyway, what are you doing still walking around with a picture of *her?* I mean if you're gonna give up golf, give the sticks away.

JERRY. (*Amused.*) You're angry about something.

GITTEL. (*All in one sentence.*) I am not angry about anything why didn't you tell me about the divorce?

JERRY. Oh! . . . She told you.

GITTEL. You think she called up to give me a recipe? . . . Why didn't you tell me, Jerry? I know we don't discuss your law journals a lot but divorces I'm interested in.

JERRY. I don't know . . . I had to live with it a bit longer, I guess.

GITTEL. You didn't want me to know. Maybe you *never* wanted me to know . . . But it's okay to tell her all about me . . . (*He moves toward her.*) Don't touch me. (*She sits.*)

JERRY. I *had* to tell her, Gittel.

GITTEL. She's still in love with you, you know.

JERRY. She didn't tell you that.

GITTEL. She didn't have to. I could hear it in her voice . . . She coulda dialed a wrong number, I could still tell.

JERRY. All the more reason for me not to hurt her now.

GITTEL. And how about what hurts me? Like when you get a divorce and it's a secret between the two of you! My God, one of these days you'll finally marry me and she'll know it and I won't! (*She grabs dance bag, starts for door.*)

JERRY. Where are you going?

GITTEL. I got a rehearsal, get out of my way.

JERRY. You're not leaving like this, Gittel.

GITTEL. I am warning you Jerry. Get out of my way or I'll let you have it!

JERRY. Sit down, Gittel!

GITTEL. *Get out of my way!* (*And she hits him as hard as she can.*) Now will you move?

JERRY. (*Softly.*) No.

GITTEL. (*Collapsing in tears.*) Sonofabitch, in all my life I could never beat up one goddam man, it's no fair!

JERRY. I was wrong not to tell you about the decree, Gittel, and I'm sorry. I would have told you tonight after the concert, you can believe that or not as you please. (*Starting for his coat.*) . . . Now I'm going to see Tess. I'm going to find out why she's here and send her back. I'll come to the concert from there. (*Stopping at door.*) Gittel . . .

GITTEL. (*Her voice muffled.*) What?

JERRY. Still friends? (*A long pause, then . . .*)

GITTEL. Still friends.

JERRY. See you at the concert. (*He exits Left.*)

(*The lights fade,* JERRY'S APARTMENT *clears. MUSIC up, and a sharp seque to THE CONCERT which we see from backstage. The Proscenium Arch is Up Stage, and the Wings and Portals of the Theatre are Down Stage.* DAVID *enters from Right, and nervously watches his* DANCERS *perform THE CONCERT, encouraging them with stage-whispered ad libs: "Smile Tommy. No, not at me, at them!" "Sail, Don, with your long legs" "Point your toes, kids, pointed toes are in!", etc. At the end of THE CONCERT there is much pre-recorded Applause, and the* DANCE COMPANY *takes their bows. Two or three come back through the Curtain, grab* DAVID, *and bring him Up Stage through the Curtain for his bow. The* KIDS *and* GITTEL *come back, leaving* DAVID *Up Stage. During the excited ad libs by the* KIDS, SOPHIE *enters along with* WELLWISHERS *and crosses to* GITTEL.)

SOPHIE. Where is she? Where is she? (*Seeing* GITTEL.) . . . Prima ballerina! (*And she runs into* GITTEL'S *arms.*) Git, it was beautiful! They loved it! Didn't you hear them yelling "encore" and "bravo, Mosca"?

GITTEL. Yeah, I recognized your voice.

SOPHIE. I couldn't stop myself! And hey, was that David talking to whom I *think* he was talking to right now whom

I also happened to notice sitting in the first row looking *most*
impressed throughout?

GITTEL. It's him all right. I recognized him from his pic-
tures! He sent a note back asking to see David for a minute.
David's with him right now, so keep your fingers crossed . . .
(*Looking around.*) . . . Uh, you alone?

SOPHIE. (*A deep breath, leveling with her.*) Yeah, Git.
Jerry never picked up his ticket. (*Then brightly.*) . . . But
don't feel bad, he mighta' had a good excuse, maybe he was
hit by a taxi!

GITTEL. No such luck. Probably that goddam office. You
know how it is, some important client comes in from out-of-
town and Jerry gets stuck with him! He's probably down
there right now arguing about some goddam statute. Listen,
I practically expected this, boy, lawyers . . .

(*Through this THE CONCERT has been moved Off Stage.
DAVID has come through the Curtain with a dazed look on
his face. At this point SOPHIE and GITTEL clear, leaving
DAVID on a bare stage.*)

DAVID. He liked it! He liked it! He really liked it! He
said: "Would you be interested in assisting me on my new
Broadway show?" and I said: "Gee, I'm not really interested
in being an *assistant* choreographer." I am lying, I am lying,
I am lying . . . I *really* said: "Interested? Interested? Would
I be *interested!?*" (*He runs madly around the stage, whooping
loudly and somehow magically triggering bright, multi-colored
lights, all this accompanied by building MUSIC. Suddenly he
stops dead Center.*) Well, it's a beginning. (*He sings.*)

IT'S NOT WHERE YOU START
IT'S WHERE YOU FINISH
IT'S NOT HOW YOU GO
IT'S HOW YOU LAND.
A HUNDRED-TO-ONE SHOT
YOU CALL HIM A KLUTZ
CAN OUTRUN THE FAV'RITE
ALL HE NEEDS IS THE GUTS.
YOUR FINAL RETURN WILL NOT DIMINISH
AND YOU CAN BE THE CREAM OF THE CROP
IT'S NOT WHERE YOU START
IT'S WHERE YOU FINISH
AND YOU'RE GONNA FINISH ON TOP!

(DAVID *dances, and is soon joined by* OTHERS *as they sing, parading around stage in fanciful balloon costumes.*)

OTHERS.
IT'S NOT WHERE YOU START
IT'S WHERE YOU FINISH
  DAVID.
NOT WHERE YOU START
IT'S WHERE YOU FINISH
  OTHERS.
IT'S NOT HOW YOU GO
IT'S HOW YOU LAND
  DAVID.
NOT HOW YOU GO
IT'S HOW YOU LAND
  (*Dance section.*)
YOUR FINAL RETURN WILL NOT DIMINISH
AND YOU CAN BE THE CREAM OF THE CROP
  ALL.
IT'S NOT WHERE YOU START
IT'S WHERE YOU FINISH
AND YOU'RE GONNA FINISH ON TOP!
  (*Dance section, including an elaborate stair climbing number that* DAVID *executes.*)
IF YOU START AT THE TOP
YOU'RE CERTAIN TO DROP
YOU'VE GOT TO WATCH YOUR TIMING
BETTER BEGIN BY CLIMBING
UP, UP, UP THE LADDER

IF YOU'RE GOING TO LAST
YOU CAN'T MAKE IT FAST, MAN
NOBODY STARTS A WINNER
GIVE ME A SLOW BEGINNER

EASY DOES IT MY FRIEND
CONSERVE YOUR FINE ENDURANCE
EASY DOES IT MY FRIEND
FOR THAT'S YOUR LIFE INSURANCE
WHILE YOU ARE YOUNG
TAKE IT RUNG AFTER RUNG AFTER RUNG
    AFTER RUNG
AFTER RUNG AFTER RUNG AFTER RUNG
    AFTER RUNG!

(*And* DAVID *ascends the stairs, exiting Stage Left. A Dance*

is performed by the OTHERS. *Then* DAVID *pokes his head
out from the top of the Step Unit.)*

DAVID. Wait . . . (*Positioning himself on the top step,
equipped with a white top hat.*) Now! (*And the* OTHERS *start
singing again, as he descends the stairs, throwing confetti
from his top hat.*)

OTHERS.

IT'S NOT WHERE YOU START
IT'S WHERE YOU FINISH! WOW!
IT'S NOT HOW YOU GO
IT'S HOW YOU LAND
A HUNDRED-TO-ONE SHOT
YOU CALL HIM A KLUTZ
CAN OUTRUN THE FAV'RITE
ALL HE NEEDS IS THE GUTS
YOUR FINAL RETURN WILL NOT DIMINISH
AND YOU CAN BE THE CREAM OF THE CROP
IT'S NOT WHERE YOU START
IT'S WHERE YOU FINISH
AND YOU'RE GONNA FINISH ON. . . .

DAVID. Wait! Come back . . . we've got to do a bigger
finish . . .

(*The* OTHERS, *who were in the process of exiting, return for
the big ending, resplendent with balloons, streamers, confetti, lights, high-kicks, etc.*)

ALL.

IT'S NOT WHERE YOU START
IT'S WHERE YOU FINISH
IT'S NOT WHERE YOU START
IT'S WHERE YOU FINISH
IT'S NOT WHERE YOU START
IT'S WHERE YOU FINISH
IT'S NOT WHERE YOU START
IT'S WHERE YOU FINISH
AND YOU'RE GONNA FINISH ON
TOP!

(*At the end of the Number, there is a ride-out in which*
DAVID *leads the* OTHERS *off.*)

IT'S NOT HOW YOU START
IT'S HOW YOU FINISH
IT'S NOT HOW YOU GO
IT'S HOW YOU LAND
IT'S NOT HOW YOU GO

IT'S HOW YOU FINISH
AND YOU'RE GONNA FINISH
ON TOP!
YOU'RE GONNA FINISH ON TOP!

(*The* OTHERS *exit.* DAVID *is then handed a broom from Stage
Right. He resignedly sweeps away the lights, confetti, and
finally one last little TWINKLETOE DANCER, Stage
Left. End Number, and we follow* DAVID *and* GITTEL
*as they walk home through CENTRAL PARK. A Park
Bench, glides to Center Stage. A light snow has begun to
fall, and* GITTEL *says . . .)*

GITTEL. Hey, you know what I feel like? Graduation. Like
I'm sitting in the auditorium all proud and you're up there
in one of those black things with a cardboard hat. You did
it, David. You really did it.

DAVID. No, Gittel, *we* did it, us! And you're gonna be right
there with me as soon as I can work it out . . . I mean look,
why can't the assistant have an assistant?

GITTEL. (*Shaking her head.*) I don't think so, David. I
been thinking about it a lot lately, how I feel about dancing
. . . it just doesn't happen anymore . . .

DAVID. What doesn't happen? What are you talking about?
You're a dancer. Dancing is your whole life!

GITTEL. Yeah, eighteen years and I am no where near where
I thought I'd be. But don't feel bad about it because there
is something else my life is! I don't know what yet . . . But
I'm gonna find out. (*Then brightly.*) . . . Anyhow when Jerry
passes his Bar who's gonna have time for classes? He won't
have money for a secretary at first so it'll probably be me! I
can take shorthand and brush up on my typing, listen it
won't do any harm, a secretary can always make a good liv-
ing . . . (*Pulling herself back.*) Geez, what's the matter with
me, one o'clock in the morning in the snow and I'm giving a
lecture on Speedwriting! I better let you go home. (*She puts
out her hand.*) . . . Bye, David.

DAVID. Cut it out, Gittel! You say goodbye like it was goodbye or something! The show rehearses here and when it goes
out of town, it's only for a couple of months. We're us, together, like always. Besides, you're gonna take care of the
studio . . .

GITTEL. What studio? There's no more studio . . . they
come because you teach, not because I'm there. You're gonna
be a big choreographer. Listen, it's *graduation*. (DAVID *looks*

at her for a moment then grabs his dance bag, and yells as he runs off Stage Right.)

DAVID. *I love you Gittel Mosca!*

(*The Park Bench is struck. An AIRPORT PHONE BOOTH appears Stage Right. JERRY walks up to it and dials. GITTEL's phone starts ringing in HER APARTMENT, as it glides in Stage Left. She slowly enters and goes to answer it.*)

GITTEL. Yeah, hello? . . . Hello? (*Nothing.*) Look is anyone there or are you one of those nuts and if you are don't waste your time I know more dirty words than you do!

JERRY. Gittel . . .

GITTEL. Jerry?

JERRY. I'm sorry about the concert. I called the theatre an hour ago but they said you'd gone.

GITTEL. Yeah, it was a big success so we went out to celebrate. You . . . you still at the hotel?

JERRY. No, I'm at the airport, Gittel. Tess was in pretty bad shape, so I waited 'til she calmed down and put her on the first flight to Omaha. That's why I didn't make it.

GITTEL. Oh, I wasn't worried . . . I knew it was something important. What was she in bad shape about?

JERRY. Me, Gittel. She still loves me.

GITTEL. So what else is new? I mean we all love you, you're some popular guy. Only who does Jerry love?

JERRY. Gittel . . . please . . .

GITTEL. No, Jerry, who do you love? Just say it once and for all, then we'll all know.

JERRY. Can't we talk about this tomorrow? . . .

GITTEL. No, Jerry, we can't! You see I'm not some cool blonde Wasp lady who can smile and keep her big mouth shut; I'm one of your hot-blooded Biblical broads and I don't sleep on a fight . . . I slug it out now! So you said I'm a gift, big deal! Only it's the kind you keep the tag on and return two days after Christmas! Well, that's not good enough for me, Jerry, I don't want to be sent back or stood up or stepped on by any more so just watch your eardrums 'cause I'm slamming down this phone! You watching? (*And she does. Instant regret, she picks up the phone.*) . . . Jerry, wait a minute. Jerry! (*Dialing.*) Hello Information, gimme the airport. Whadda'ya' mean *what* airport, the one that goes to Omaha! All right then the pay phone at Kennedy. How many? Four hundred and sixty-two . . . Business must be pretty good. Never mind operator. I'll wait in case he calls me . . . (*She listens for a second.*) . . . Yeah, a man . . . you too? . . . no kidding . . . The dirty bastard . . . Geez, that's rough . . . four kids, hah? . . . you wasted eleven years . . . (*The lights dim,* JERRY *enters* GITTEL'S APARTMENT. *He crosses and sits on the bed, she is on the sofa. He is still wearing his coat. Lights up.*) . . . What should I be mad about? I'm glad you came over. Okay, are you ready?

JERRY. Go ahead.

GITTEL. (*Taking a deep breath.*) Okay, Jerry, you once said we were friends, right? And a friend gotta right to say anything he wants to a friend so I'm gonna. Jerry, I love you. I'm not ashamed to say it, I love you and I want you. And I gotta know if you're ever gonna be able to say that about me! I'll give it to you straight, Jer. You stay with me and I'll never let up on you marrying me. I'll be at you day and night. So if you're my friend, you gotta give it to me straight, too.

JERRY. All right Gittel, here it is straight. You and I say the word "love" . . . and I think we mean different things.

GITTEL. I mean wanting someone . . . so bad . . .

JERRY. So do I, Gittel! I know what it is to want someone, to have them, to be with your lover in every conceivable way . . . And that's a part of love. But then there's something else that happens between two people. Something that comes after years of giving, taking, exchanging . . . of being friends *and* enemies. Of being brave together, Gittel . . . and being scared to death, too! Gittel, it's something that grows between two people, and *attaches* them to each other, so that if one of them happens to like . . . bridges . . . you never see one goddamn bridge except through her eyes! And finally that person becomes a part of you, your arms, your hand, and you can't cut it off without dying a little yourself! That's it straight, Gittel. That's what love is to me.

GITTEL. And that kind of loving . . . with the bridges stuff . . . I can't get from you. So how do I compete, Jerry? Have a hemorrhage twice a year?

JERRY. I said it before and I meant it, Gittel. As long as you need me I'll be here.

GITTEL. My God, I'm in a goddam trap! If I need him he stays but only because I need him! Why, Jerry? What's in it for you?

JERRY. One of the two things I want most, Gittel. To see you fulfilled . . .

GITTEL. And what's the other thing, Jerry? (*He doesn't answer.*) . . . What's the other thing, Jerry?

JERRY. (*Finally.*) Tess. I want the same thing for her.

GITTEL. (*Her eyes blinking.*) . . . Well, how do you like that, that's practically what I was hoping it was. Because I've been doing a lot of thinking and I don't want just part of anybody anymore. I got a right to have one hundred percent of some guy for myself and until I find someone who'll say all that bridge stuff about me, I'm not settling! (*Then softly.*) So I guess we call it off, huh?

JERRY. What is this, Gittel? Another handout?

GITTEL. Yeah. But for me this time . . . Jerry, Jerry . . . would you go? I'd like to be alone. I'd like to be alone. (*The lights fade on* GITTEL'S APARTMENT. *Music of "SEESAW" comes up and* JERRY'S APARTMENT *comes on to meet* GITTEL'S . . . *Lights come up on* JERRY'S APARTMENT *as he is dialing the phone. The phone rings in* GITTEL'S APARTMENT. *The lights come up on* GITTEL *as she answers the phone.*) Yeah, hello?

JERRY. Gittel, I'm all packed so . . .

GITTEL. Hiya, Jerry.

JERRY. I left some cartons of odds and ends in the kitchen, the janitor's got the key if there's anything you want.

GITTEL. I don't want anything.

JERRY. If you do. And if anything comes up I'll be at the Commodore Hotel in Lincoln. That's Lincoln Nebraska, not Nevada.

GITTEL. Not Nevada.

JERRY. As soon as I get an office and a phone I'll send you the number. If you need anything before then . . .

GITTEL. Oh, I don't need anything. I'm all right now, Jerry. You just get what you want out there, huh?

JERRY. I'll try. My terms are steep. I won't work for my father-in-law and I won't live in Omaha. All we'll have is what I earn. Tess understands that. It's a new deal for both of us.

GITTEL. I'm rooting for you, Jerry.

JERRY. I'm rooting for you too. It's a big city, he's bound to be around some corner. Just don't give up on him.

GITTEL. I won't! You know me, I bounce up like . . . like a jack-in-the-box. Besides I got a better opinion of myself now. I'm gonna propose more often. Anyhow, it's in the air. Guess who just got married . . . Soph! The King! He gave up his throne for the woman he loved . . . (*Softly.*) . . . I'll send you a birthday card now and then, huh?

JERRY. Now and then.

GITTEL. (*Before she can stop herself.*) Twice a week!

JERRY. (*Shaken.*) Gittel, what am I doing, I . . .

GITTEL. No Jerry, you're doing right! I don't want any handouts either! You taught me that. I want somebody'll take care of me who's all mine. And nobody like Wally or Oscar

either, between them they couldn't take care of a Chiclet.
Things look different to me now, Jerry. You did me a world of
good.

JERRY. Did I, Gittel? I'd like to think that.

GITTEL. Sure! I mean it's the first affair I came out with
more than I went in! Whoever this guy is, Jerry, he'll owe
you.

JERRY. Tess'll owe you, Gittel. More than she'll ever know.
Just don't forget who you are, Gittel! I promise you I never
will. (*Then.*) . . . Goodbye, Gittel.

GITTEL. Goodbye, Jerry. (*Then suddenly, unable to stop
herself.*) . . . I love you, Jerry! Long as you live I want you
to remember the last thing you heard out of me was I love
you! (*A long silence, then* JERRY *speaks.*)

JERRY. I love you too, Gittel. (*And he hangs up. A second's
pause then he starts for his suitcase.* GITTEL *has meanwhile
frantically dialed his number.* JERRY *is at the door when phone
rings. He stops, the phone rings twice, then* GITTEL *suddenly
puts down receiver. The phone stops ringing.* JERRY *is released.
He exits. Lights down on* JERRY'S APARTMENT, *Music up, as*
GITTEL *walks to the bed, picks up the pink flamingo and looks
at it. She reprises "LOVABLE LUNATIC." Listening to the
words as she sings them, she begins to understand them for the
first time.*)

GITTEL.
YOU'RE A LOVABLE LUNATIC
AN IMPOSSIBLE CASE
BUT I'M QUEER FOR LUNATICS
'SPECIALLY A LUNATIC
WITH A LOVABLE FACE. . . .
AN INCREDIBLE MANIAC
YOU'RE SO FIERCELY INTENSE
BUT WHATEVER YOU DO
IS SO RIGHT AND SO TRUE
THAT SOMEHOW IT MAKES SENSE
> (GITTEL *throws down the flamingo, grabs her coat and,
> hurriedly putting it on, crosses to Up Stage Center. The
> two* APARTMENTS *split and are struck, then the Pro-
> jection Screens fly in with thousands of lights of the
> New York skyline. She crosses Down to Center.*)

Lovable? Eegh! A lunatic? Yes!
> (*And she sings.*)

I MUST HAVE BEEN OUT OF MY MIND!
I MUST HAVE BEEN OUT OF MY BOX!

I REALLY BELIEVED I WOULD HAVE AN AFFAIR
THAT WOULDN'T END UP ON THE ROCKS!
    (*Talking to herself.*)
Ha! What a laugh!
    (*She laughs.*)
So who's laughing?

    (*She sings.*)
TEN MINUTES AGO HE SAID: "I LOVE YOU"
THE FIRST AND ONLY TIME HE SAID: "I LOVE
    YOU"
TEN MINUTES AGO HE SAID: "I LOVE YOU"
THE FIRST AND ONLY TIME HE SAID: "I LOVE
    YOU"
HE SAID: "I LOVE YOU"
HE SAID: "I LOVE YOU"
HE SAID: "I LOVE YOU"
HE SAID: "I LOVE YOU"
HE SAID HE LOVED ME
I WAS LOST UNTIL HE FOUND ME
WHY DO I STILL FEEL HIS STRONG ARMS
    AROUND ME?
SINGLE NIGHTS IN A DOUBLE BED ALONE
AND I'LL MISS YOUR FINGERS
TOUCHING EACH EROGENOUS ZONE!
I'LL MISS YOU, JERRY RYAN
DAMN YOU, DAMN YOU, JERRY RYAN
I LOVE YOU, JERRY RYAN!
THOUGH IT'S YOU I MUST FORGET
I CAN'T LET MYSELF REGRET IT
I'M WAY AHEAD. . . .
SO THAT'S THAT, I LOVED, I LOST
WHAT'S A HEART? THAT'S ALL IT COST ME
I'M WAY AHEAD. . . .

MY CHIN IS UP!
MY HANDS ARE STEADY NOW
COME ON, NEW DREAM
NEW LIFE, I'M READY NOW!

WHEN I THINK OF EVERY NIGHT
EVEN NIGHTS WHEN WE WERE FIGHTING
I'M WAY AHEAD. . . .
ONCE YOU SAID THE WAY TO LIVE
WAS TO TAKE AS WELL AS GIVE
WELL SAID, WELL SAID. . . .

GOODBYE, GOOD LUCK
I SEE NOW
WHAT LOVE LIKE YOURS CAN BE, NOW
THANK YOU. . . .
JERRY. . . .

EV'RYBODY'S TRAVELLIN' ON A CRAZY
SEESAW!
LOVE IS UP. . . . DOWN
UP. . . . DOWN
AS MY LIFE GOES BY
I'LL FIND MYSELF A GUY FOR THE
SEESAW
SEESAW
A NEW FELLA FOR THE SEESAW
THERE'S GOTTA BE TWO FOR THE SEESAW. . . .
TWO FOR THE SEESAW. . . .
AND SO I KNOW I'M GONNA GO EV'RYWHERE
I KNOW I'M GONNA FIND EV'RYTHING
I'LL TELL IT TO ANYONE ANYWHERE
THAT LOVE IS A HELL OF A RIDE
ONE HELL OF A RIDE!
    (*Curtain.*)

END OF PLAY

(*Curtain rises on* FULL COMPANY *taking bows and reprising*
   "*IT'S NOT WHERE YOU START*.")

   FULL COMPANY.
IT'S NOT WHERE YOU START
IT'S WHERE YOU FINISH
IT'S NOT HOW YOU GO
IT'S HOW YOU LAND
A HUNDRED-TO-ONE SHOT
YOU CALL HIM A KLUTZ
CAN OUTRUN THE FAV'RITE
ALL HE NEEDS IS THE GUTS

YOUR FINAL RETURN WILL NOT DIMINISH
AND YOU CAN BE THE CREAM OF THE CROP
IT'S NOT WHERE YOU START
IT'S WHERE YOU FINISH
AND YOU'RE GONNA FINISH ON. . . .

(*Final curtain.* ORCHESTRA *reprises* "*SEESAW*" *as Exit Music*
   for House.)

PROPERTY LIST

STAGE LEFT:

Preset:

1. Make up 11 sets of 3 balloons each—red, green, blue, or yellow combination on strings with elastic loops.

1A. White balloon on top hat with confetti—get from Tommy Tune.

2. Food:
   1 tuna sandwich on rye
   1 pot mushroom soup
   1 tray with:
       4 old fashioned glasses—coke
       1 pilsner glass—water
       1 pilsner glass—orange juice
       1 pilsner glass—coke
       1 glass each—regular milk—thin mixture powdered milk

3. Gittel No. 1
   Bed with:
       2 sheets
       2 pillow cases
       spread
       blanket—folded, pinned to spread
       telephone on bed table (long cord, top drawer dresser)
       atomizer on dresser—stockings in dresser drawer
       lighter fluid can (water), top drawer bed stand
       telephone book (Manhattan) on bed stand
       milk carton half full thin mixture—top shelf of refrigerator
       coffee mug no. 1, spoon on refrigerator
       pill bottle on refrigerator
       sofa—two pillows
       "Dance" picture above Stage Left end of sofa
       mirror on sliding door

Dressing Props:
   pussy willows on waste basket Stage Left end of sofa
   2 paper butterflies, 1 "smile" button
   coathooks, "incense" lamp—pictures
   spice rack, pot holders, dish towels, trivet in kitchen

4. Preset Desk unit pallette in track on dog
   desk with wastebasket attached
   telephone (black)
   ledger
   bills
   rubber stamp, stamp pad, calendar stamp

5. Preset restaurant unit
   table
   2 cushions

candle
2 menus
2 napkins
2 sets chopsticks
1 teapot
2 teacups

6. Set party wagon (from "Hamlet" wagon storage to No. 2 Stage Left)
1 ashtray, 1 pack cigarettes
1 disposable type lighter
7. conga drum Stage Left

RUNNING ORDER

Top of "Nobody Does It Like Me"—start heating soup
Jerry's second phone call—"Meet me at Broadway and 46th"—strike
    desk pallette to Stage Left storage.
Immediately preset *waitress* tray in "1."
Pick up on her exit.
Clear restaurant unit when it comes off.

Set Gittel No. 2— As soon as unit comes off "Holiday Inn"
    strike blanket, remake bed
    blue dress on sofa
    red, green, light blue dresses on bed
    pants suit hangs in closet
    no. 2 coffee mug to coffee table
    strike no. 1 coffee mug and spoon
    stockings hanging out of bureau drawer
    close door

Set party units—"dressing" scene
    2 pallettes with 1 table, 2 stools, 2 glasses coke
    tray with 3 pilsner glasses to "Hamlet" wagon
    large party wagon with 1 table, 4 stools Upstage of Gittel
    unit track (when Gittel unit comes off, set wagon in track on dog)
"Ride Out the Storm"—Set Gittel's No. 3
    long cord on telephone—on sofa (cord in top drawer of bureau)
    bed pillow to sofa
    pills to coffee table (from top of refrigerator)
    real milk in mug on coffee table
INTERMISSION
    Gittel's—strike clothing from bed
    coffee mug no. 1 with spoon to top of refrigerator
    pill bottle to top of refrigerator
    strike long cord from phone—phone to coffee table
    strike coffee mug no. 2, milk carton
    no. 2 bird to bed
    set hospital beds to spike marks
    Stage Left bed has traction unit, sling, cast
    "Everybody Else"—strike hospital beds as they come off
        (sandwich bag to Stage Right)

"Not Where You Start"—Top hat with balloon and confetti to
  Tommy Tune on cue from Stage Manager
Gittell No. 3—Close kitchen door from Upstage on cue. (Blackout,
  "Would you go, I want to be alone.")

Stage Left Prop Table:
  hot plate
  saucepan
  dish soap—paper towels
  dresses—1 green, 1 red, 1 blue-green
  1 black pants suit on padded hanger
  no. 2 coffee cup
  no. 2 bird
  restaurant order pad, pencil
  waitress tray with tuna sandwich, bowl hot soup
  china spoon, fake milk glass, 1 set chopsticks
  conga drum

Supplies:
  1 gross each—red, green, blue, yellow, white balloons
  1 tank helium with valve, balloon string, elastic loops, plastic rings
    (three-quarter inch)
  confetti—2 boxes, 50 packages each—multicolored
  chopsticks—16 pairs
  Kent cigarettes
  paper towels, dish soap

Food per week:
  1 lb. tuna salad
  2 loaves rye bread
  1 quart orange juice
  1 quart milk
  8 cans Coke
  8 cans mushroom soup
  1 small box Carnation powdered milk

Preset:
  Jerry No. 1—orange crate pallette and chairs
  paper towels on refrigerator
  bottle of wine (under sink)
  wall shelf (with condiments)
  1 wood chest (3 mugs on top)
  1 kitchen window drape
  2 soup plates (with 3 knives and 3 forks) on back burner of gas stove
  1 soup plate (with 2 pot holders) on front burner
  small shelf (bathroom wall) with 5 bottles (pepper, etc.)
  1 plastic pitcher with leaves (on bathtub)
  kitchen towel on hook (next to sink)
  roll of paper towels (over sink)

Preset:
  N.Y. Phone booth (in first entrance)
  1 white push broom (in first entrance)
  4 glasses ("Ride Out the Storm")

casserole with beans (on second front burner)
"Burnt Thing" (at end of "Holiday Inn")
    Line is: "I have appointment with Lawyer."
(*Dry Ice* into tepid water and set in stove)
warm up beans and water in pot at start of show
have small package of dry ice ready (each performance)
have two pallettes ready with two tables and 4 stools (Offstage Right)

Preset *Jerry's No. 2* (at intermission—switch phone booths)

Set:
    2 wall easels
    Jerry's suitcase
    Flamingo (stork)
    2 champagne bottles
    2 fruit baskets
    3 fake bouquets (hospital scene)
    2 candy boxes
    3 champagne glasses

Off Stage Right:
    1 empty carton (some junk in it and Gittel's picture on top)
    1 toy gun (pistol type)
    6 small trays of groceries
    push pins (for Gittel's picture)
    Tommy Tune's small trunk to his dresser

ACT ONE—(Moves)
    telephone booth (On on Stage Manager's cue)
    telephone booth (Off on Stage Manager's cue)

Preset dry ice (in oven) after Gittel's song, "Holiday Inn"
    (Cue Line: "I know a lawyer in this town")

Jerry's No. 1 on—then after dinner scene—off
    strike all dressing *except* phone

INTERMISSION

Preset hospital gifts on Stage Center:
    2 bouquets, 2 candy boxes, 3 champagne glasses and 2 champagne
    bottles

Off Stage Right—Dress Jerry's No. 2 fully:
    3 drapes, etc. all shelves
    sink drape
    2 wall shelves with madeup groceries
    kitchen table pallette replaces crate pallette

Reset:
    Banana bowl with bananas
    roll of paper towels
    pitcher of flowers
    (apartment is fully dressed)

NOTE: When this unit comes off during Act Two, strike all drapes,
    leaves, paper towel roll, banana bowl and groceries and preset for
    Jerry's Apartment No. 3.

Preset:
    1 suitcase (on kitchen table)
    coke carton (on refrigerator)
    cardboard carton (on bathtub)
    bar unit—tray with 12 glasses, filled

Off Stage Right Props:
    bananas
    canned beans (1 each performance)
    grape juice (wine)
    pot of water
    hot plate (2 burner)
    2 pot holders
    4 water (coca-cola) glasses
    3 kitchen towels and roll of paper towels
    dry ice (keep in refrigerator)
    wash basin and ivory liquid

INTERMISSION:
    thermometer
    paper bags(take sandwich)
    keep Gittel's picture in 1st entrance

ACT TWO—(Moves)
No. 1 End-Hospital Scene (Actors bring all gifts off—STORE)
No. 2 End of Jerry's No. 2
    strike apartment scene—bare
    set suitcase (on kitchen table)
    set empty coke carton (on refrigerator)
    set empty carton (on bathtub)
No. 5 Get suitcase from John Gavin
No. 6 Strike kitchen table pallette (for boys)

IMPORTANT!
Order:
    2 compressed air tanks with nozzle for balloons
    1 tank of helium with nozzle for balloons

COSTUME PLOT

GITTLE:
  2 red and white shirts
  1 body stocking with mike and batteries
  black tights
  black trunks
  beige tights
  appliqued levis
  plain levis
  grey sweatshirt
  2 faded blue denim shirts
  blue and white stripe jersey shirt (salt)
  magenta sweater
  fur trimmed floral cut velvet coat
  green tie-dyed velvet gown
  red feather boa
  dark green V-neck pullover sweater
  off white matte jersey blouse
  white hospital gown
  navy banlon shirt
  navy wool pants
  navy collar with ribbon
  navy gloves
  2 tan leather shoulder bags

Prop gowns:
  1 chiffon off-beige gown
  1 red wool sheath
  1 halter top green satin gown
  1 black, open navel "pants suit" (one piece)
  1 blue terry cloth bathrobe
  2 pink slippers
  1 navy slip-on pumps (concert)
  1 pair beige grasshoppers
  white sox
  1 white/lavender print silk Spanglish Scarf

JERRY:
  3 white dress shirts
  3 white pleated front evening shirts
  3 white button down shirts
  3 light blue shirts
  3 yellow short sleeve pullover shirts
  2 maroon long sleeve cotton jersey shirts
  1 grey knitted wool 2 piece suit
  1 blue serge 3 piece suit

1 grey wool slacks
1 blue pinstripe wool 3 piece suit
2 pair shoes—black
3 neckties
4 pair black sox

SOPHIE:
2 green helenca body shirts
1 pair yellow shorts
silver chain belt
purple handkerchief
black English net gown with black and silver bugle bead design
black silk slip
black and purple batwing wraparound blouse
black jersey long pants
green gros-grain head band
black cape
silver shoes

SPARKLE:
1 white shirt, silver ruffles
1 pair grey satin bell bottom pants
1 silver lame coat, rhinestone trim
1 pair red shoes

JULIO GONZALES:
1 pair brown polyester pants
1 purple sweat shirt

Ensemble Costume Sets
1. Opening—white set
13 assorted ladies outfits, shoes, miscellaneous accessories
14 mens outfits, shoes
(also some play in Hospital Scene and all in finale)
2. 6 Ladies Hookers Costumes, shoes
2 pair brown, 2 orange, 2 gold pair hose
3 garter belts, 1 whip
3. Policeman
short sleeve shirt, badge
black pants, belt
holster belt, night stick
police hat
black shoes
3—muggers
1. Berdahl
brown corduroy pants
brown raincoat
grey checked hat
2. Swiggard
green raincoat
brown pants
leatherette cap

3. Alubey
   brown wool shirt
   tan V-neck sweater
   grey hat
   (doubles Spanglish pants)
4. Spanglish
   13 ladies yellow blouses
   13 ladies black with silver study shorts or skirts
   2 pair ladies black trunks
   13 mens yellow satin shirts
   12 mens black silver studded levis
   1 mens black plain levis
   26 purple handkerchiefs
   13 pair ladies orange shoes
   13 pair mens orange shoes or boots
5. Ride Out the Storm
   11 ladies red costumes, shoes
   13 mens red/purple costumes, shoes
   2 sparkelette costumes—silver fringe on pants and bras, wrist hangings
6. Hospital Scene (Repeats many opening costumes)
   1 pair striped pajamas
   2 Nurses white uniforms
   1 Nurses Aid—white blouse, blue/white stripe pinafore
   7 mens white lab coats
7. Ballet Class and Jazz Class
   6 ladies green tops, assorted
   6 ladies green tights and trunks
   3 mens green tights
   7 mens green or white shirts
   7 mens green or beige wool pants
8. The Concert and Not Where You Start
   10 ladies banlon navy long sleeve shirts
   9 mens banlon navy long sleeve shirts
   9 ladies navy wool pants
   9 mens navy wool pants
   9 mens, 9 ladies black or navy character shoes
   10 ladies, 9 mens navy gloves
   8 ladies, 8 mens navy velveteen collars with hanging ribbons
   9 mens navy T-shirts
   8 ladies balloon capes
   8 mens black elastic balloon belts
   17 navy top hats with colored wigs attached
   16 navy top hats (with balloons, to go on top of wig hats)
   1 balloon tutu foundation (B. Lee)

OTHER TITLES AVAILABLE FROM SAMUEL FRENCH

ANGRY HOUSEWIVES
A.M. Collins and Chad Henry

Musical / 4m, 4f / Various sets

Bored with their everyday lives and kept in insignificance by their boyfriends/husbands, these are four angry women. They try a number of outlets, but nothing suits until one of them strikes a chord on her guitar and suggests that they form a punk rock group to enter the upcoming talent show at the neighborhood punk club. Their group "The Angry Housewives," enter and win. This genial satire of contemporary feminism ran for ages in Seattle and has had numerous successful productions across the country.

"The show is insistently outrageous, frequently funny, occasionally witty and altogether irresistible."
– *Seattle Times*

SAMUELFRENCH.COM

Lightning Source UK Ltd.
Milton Keynes UK
UKOW030815060213

205883UK00007B/121/P